About the Author

Dan Brown, 53, was born in County Durh northeast of England. From the age of six, 1 with his family, gaining a deep appreciatic variety of cultures around the world.

His interest in writing began when he found a signed book by Rudyard Kipling in his family home that inspired Dan to wonder whether his own words might one day outlive him, too.

Now living in Doncaster with his wife, Dan continues to write and explore. He believes that the pursuit of life experiences holds far more value than the accumulation of possessions, and he dedicates his spare time to travelling the world, always seeking new stories to tell.

Introduction

Jack Crane was two cups into a bitter morning when the email arrived.

The rain had returned — that slow, directionless drizzle that turned London's bricks into blotting paper. His flat smelled of instant coffee and damp notebooks. He sat hunched at the desk beneath a shelf lined with old press badges and unpaid freelance invoices, half-listening to the static murmur of the BBC through a cracked speaker.

The subject line was terse:

URGENT — Richat Structure Commission

He almost deleted it on instinct. The Richat Structure? That spiral thing in Mauritania? A geological oddity cooked up by wind, water and too much internet speculation. The Eye of the Sahara. A favourite among conspiracy theorists and alien-finders. Hardly foreign affairs.

Then he saw who'd forwarded it.

Megan Kelly.

Senior Editor, The Reckoner. The woman who'd once told him, "You file better stories broken than most people do sober." A rare compliment from someone who bled red ink and didn't believe in praise.

Jack clicked the message.

The Gambian

Dan Brown

Contents

Acknowledgements.

Sitting on a beach in North Africa, writing this story, looking over at my very tolerant wife, filling her time while I work.

Thank you, Sal, my sweetheart, for your patience.

Having a reliable book editor is invaluable when writing books. For me, that's my mother, Valerie Griffiths. I can always rely on her literary acumen without any editorial fees to burden me.

Introduction

We need someone on the ground to investigate recent reports from Mauritania. Local archaeologists claim newly exposed petroglyphs near the Richat. Something ancient — maybe even older than the last glacial maximum. This remains unconfirmed, but we're assigning a small team to the site. You'll have local guides and official clearance through the Mauritanian Ministry of Culture. Deadline: rolling. Danger level: soft red.

He skimmed past logistics, through the pitch deck.

Stopped cold at the last line:

Team lead: Lauren Alexandra Brown

He didn't read the rest.

His eyes held on to her name like it was freshly carved.

It had been sixteen months since the end — not clean, not loud, just unfinished. She'd moved out without ceremony. No betrayal, no screaming. Just a flat suddenly empty of her boots, her voice, her presence. The last text she ever sent him read: I can't follow your ghosts anymore.

Now she wanted him on her team?

No. Megan wanted that. Lauren probably didn't know.

Jack leaned back in his chair, the springs complaining beneath him. He stared at the ceiling like it might blink.

The Richat.

A vast spiral, four hundred kilometres from anything that mattered. The kind of place you only reach if you were already half-lost. No roads. No real history. Just ancient rock weathered into something that looked too perfect, too deliberate.

A structure shaped like an eye, staring up at space.

Jack rubbed his face, the stubble rough against his palms.

He knew what this was.

Not just a job.

Not just another remote dispatch.

It was a summons.

From the past.

From a place no one could quite explain.

And, somehow, from her.

He took one last sip of cold coffee.

Then hit Reply.

I'm in.

Chapter 1

To the Eye of the Desert

The Eurostar hissed in from the tunnel, its sleek frame cutting through the hush of morning like a blade through gauze. It didn't roar. It whispered a command, as if even the machinery knew that silence preceded something sacred. The doors parted with a practised sigh.

Jack stepped aboard without a glance back.

No farewell text. No final sip of coffee. The flat was locked, the email auto-response set, the story unwritten and now irrelevant. Something deeper was stirring. Not wanderlust. Not escape.

Something old.

A pull from beneath thought, like a thread tied to his ribs and tugged by unseen fingers.

Three trains followed. Each one a little slower, a little more forgettable. Through fog-cloaked villages and windowless terminals, through passport checks where no one cared who he was. Then came the first flight. Côte d'Azur Airport Nice, France to Casablanca. Then a second—Casablanca to Nouakchott, on a plane so old the seatbelt buckle still bore a logo from a company that no longer existed.

He slept through turbulence.

Woke to sand.

The final stretch was a taxi with cracked leather seats and no meter, just a driver named Abdi who pointed once at the road and muttered, "No one builds past here. Not anymore."

Jack nodded, said nothing.

They drove in silence.

Through Nouakchott, where the buildings sagged like worn teeth, colour drained by salt wind and sun. The capital was sprawling but low, as if afraid to reach upward in a sky that no longer gave. Corrugated tin roofs shimmered. Stray goats nibbled plastic. Men sat in plastic chairs outside electronics shops that hadn't sold batteries in years.

And then: the dust.

Endless.

Heavy.

Amber in the light, and warm as breath.

Jack stepped out of the taxi.

The heat grabbed him by the collar — not violent, just possessive. He looked up.

No signs. No streets. No maps could help him now.

Jack stood in the sun-beaten dust of Nouakchott, Mauritania's low-slung capital, the air already tinged with salt and sand. A different world pressed in here—slower, drier, and built on the rhythm of things older than time.

The hotel was little more than a whitewashed block tucked down a side street, its ceiling fan wheezing like an asthmatic bird. Jack dropped his bag to the floor and pushed open the shutters. The city stretched out below him: flat rooftops, scattered date palms, and the occasional call to prayer drifting through the air like silk.

He could already feel it—the desert was near.

He took out the notebook again and wrote:

"First light in Nouakchott. There's a silence in the air like something waiting to be remembered. The wind carries more than dust. It carries names I haven't spoken in years."

Jack didn't plan on becoming a journalist—he stumbled into it by chasing the perfect frame.

He enrolled at university to study photography, drawn to it not for artistic flourish, but for its urgency: the rawness of truth captured in a single image. Jack believed the camera didn't lie. It just needed the right hands to aim it.

Downstairs, he met an old local man—a broad-shouldered man with sand-colored eyes and a voice that rasped like gravel. His name was Omar. He barely spoke, only nodded once, then showed him to the Land Cruiser that would take him into the interior.

Jack had arranged this from the UK and a mutual friend who visited the area sometimes.

His friend, Tom, had told Jack he knew a man who was willing to supply him with a vehicle for this 'quest' he had spoken about and now here he was. He paid Omar a sum of money that the old man hadn't seen all at once for many years. To Omar, the truck was sold and the money would send him in a direction he thought lost to him. To Jack, he had just hired a truck to return later.

Oh, how different cultures exist with such varied wealth.

Following some broken directions and advice, Jack set off east to Chinguetti, leaving tarmac behind, past camels chewing plastic bags and boys selling oranges in metal bowls. Soon, there were no buildings. Only sky. Only sand. Only the road ahead, curling like a dry tongue through the throat of a forgotten land.

Jack leaned his head against the glass. Somewhere beyond this stretch of earth was the Eye. The Richat Structure. The ancient ripple in the heart of the Sahara. He wasn't sure what he expected to find there—truth, perhaps. Or silence. Or maybe something he had left behind, long before he ever met Lauren.

Lauren was in his Intro to Media Ethics class. A journalism student, known for her sharp editorials in the university paper and an intolerance for lazy reporting, she asked the questions lecturers didn't want to answer. The first time Jack noticed her, she was arguing with a visiting war correspondent about Western media bias. The second time, she was calling Jack out for photographing a protest without asking people for consent.

He was intrigued. She was infuriated. They spent the next two years debating the difference between witnessing and interfering.

Eventually, they stopped debating as much and started staying up late together, piecing together stories—hers in words, his in images.

When their courses were complete, both passing with honours, Jack leaned into photojournalism. He had a gift for disappearing into the background, capturing the quiet rupture in moments of chaos: a mother shielding her child during a raid, a smuggler glancing over his shoulder mid-handshake. To Jack, photography was a big responsibility because he believed only a fraction of reality was captured with that one frame and there is a responsibility when submitting an photo, to show not just the violence, he saw that as too easy, anyone could do that but what he saw as more worthy was an image that shows the insinuation of something, that would be much more powerful and it was noticed by the agencies and papers he submitted them to.

He landed jobs quickly, thanks to Lauren's newly acquired connections and his own undeniable eye.

Together, they made a good team. She'd pitch the story, handle the interviews, and dig up the buried leads. He'd document what no one else could see. Their early work—on struggling families living in the centre of the troubles of Northern Ireland, approaching the Good Friday Agreement of 1998—got attention. Not just for the facts, but for the intimacy. The humanity.

But everything began to drift the year Jack's father, Ronnie Crane, died.

He briefly closed his eyes. And the wind whispered the first line of a memory he didn't yet recognise.

The sun hung low like a burning coin in the sky, and the road east dissolved beneath the wheels.

By late afternoon, he reached Atar, a dusty, wind-stripped town nestled in the Adrar Plateau. Jack stepped out of the truck, knees stiff from the journey, his shirt stained with sweat and sand. A haze shimmered across the earth, making even still things seem like they were breathing.

He refuelled in silence, filling plastic jerry cans from an old pump while a group of children kicked a deflated football in the red dust nearby.

Afterwards, Jack stretched his legs with a slow walk through the narrow streets, past women in bright melhfa, past market stalls piled with dates and dried fish, past goats tethered with fraying rope.

Every so often, he'd glance at his notebook but couldn't bring himself to write. Not here. Not yet.

Later that evening, in a clay-walled auberge at the edge of town, Jack ate a bowl of thieboudienne—rice and fish seasoned with garlic and lemon—sold to him by a woman cooking by the roadside for any travellers passing by hungry enough to stop. Looking around, Jack thought, 'Exactly how many people pass by here for this woman to survive on selling her cooking?' The place seemed practically deserted to him.

"Where are you heading, sir?" the woman asked.

"The Richat Structure", he replied

To Jack, she already knew what words were going to come her way.

"The Eye sees all," she said. "But it does not answer." She then muttered quietly

The next day, Chinguetti came into view by mid-afternoon—a town of sand-colored ruins and ancient silence. Once a centre of Islamic scholarship, it now stood half-buried in dunes, as if the earth itself was trying to remember what it had forgotten.

Jack wandered through the empty corridors of its oldest library, running his fingers over parchment manuscripts centuries old. He paused in front of a crumbling map drawn by hand—a rendering of the desert, with no scale and no compass, just names scratched like myths across parchment.

Near the bottom, written faintly in Arabic:

عين الصحراء – Ain al-Sahra – The Eye of the Desert.

He traced the letters with his thumb.

A soft voice spoke behind him. "You seek the Eye?"

Jack turned. A young librarian, no older than twenty-five, stood at the entrance of the room.

"Yes," Jack said. "I'm heading there tomorrow."

The young man hesitated. "The wind has changed. A storm is building in the east. The kind that doesn't pass quickly."

Jack said nothing. Part of him hoped for a sign to turn back. Another part—deeper, older—longed for the storm.

That night, he couldn't sleep. He stepped outside and climbed the low roof of the auberge. The stars above Mauritania blazed as if they had never shone anywhere else. No moon, only sky, wind, and the vast silence of a place seemingly untouched by time.

Jack took out the notebook and wrote,

"Tomorrow I go to the Eye. I don't know what I'll find. But I feel like something is waiting for me there—not a person, not a treasure. Something… older. Maybe even myself."

At dawn, he loaded the truck. No paved road this time—just tracks and instinct. The last village disappeared in the rearview mirror, and the desert opened its mouth.

Beyond that horizon, the wind began to rise.

By midday, the landscape had shifted. The ground beneath the Land Cruiser cracked and split like ancient skin, and the sun above burned white and unforgiving. There were no more signs, no more villages. Just pale sky, red rock, and the occasional skeleton of a tree that hadn't seen water in decades.

Jack shaded his eyes, peering out at the empty vastness. "How far now?" he thought.

He had always felt something in deserts—a knowing. Not nostalgia, exactly, but a sense of time thinning, like he was walking somewhere between history and myth.

And now, the wind was beginning to shift. It came in short gusts first, brushing the sand into low ribbons that danced across the path like snakes. Then came the strange silence—the kind that always comes before something big.

Jack slowed the vehicle and glanced toward the east.

On the horizon, the sky had changed. What had once been a brilliant blue was now a dull, sickly yellow. A wall of sand was gathering, rising like a mountain with no summit, moving with the slow, unstoppable power of something ancient and angry.

Jack felt his pulse quicken.

The next thirty minutes were a race against the sky. The wind howled louder now, slapping the truck with fists of sand. Visibility dropped. Shapes blurred. The air itself began to taste like grit.

Jack pulled the scarf tighter around his face. His fingers gripped the steering wheel hard as he veered off the faint track and drove toward a jagged ridge of rock in the near distance. The vehicle pitched and swayed violently across uneven terrain, the tires digging deep into the sand.

At last, he reached the base of the outcrop—a cracked sandstone overhang that jutted just enough to offer partial shelter. Jack killed the engine.

Jack climbed out and immediately felt the full force of the wind slam against him. It roared like a train, whipping his clothes, stinging his skin with sand. He dropped to a crouch and scrambled beneath a rock.

He wrapped himself in blankets and scarves, each breath a choking gasp of dust. Jack reached into his pack, fumbling, and pulled out an old black umbrella—a ridiculous object here, but something he always carried. He opened it and wedged it against the wind, using it as a makeshift shield between him and the onslaught.

Jack began smiling through this maelstrom of airborne sand. He thought to himself, "I'm in the desert, in a storm, an Englishman unprepared for all this and what do I do? I put up the umbrella Lauren left in her Backpack! I must look like a madman here now"

Then the storm fully arrived.

The world vanished. Time blurred.

Jack had no idea how long he had remained like that—huddled under a rock and umbrella, buffeted by nature's fury. Hours passed. Maybe more. The sky was gone. The earth was gone. Everything was wind and noise and movement.

He drifted in and out of consciousness, his mind latching onto fragments—Lauren's face at the window in London, the quiet streets of Chinguetti, a searing memory of walking through the Sahara years ago, alone, delirious.

Through it all, he held tightly to the notebook, now wrapped in plastic and tucked inside his jacket. It pulsed against his chest like a second heart.

Eventually—somewhere between dusk and night—the storm began to die. The roar softened to a whisper. The sand settled like ash after fire.

Jack slowly sat up, brushing himself off, blinking into a bruised orange sky. Everything around him had changed. The Land Cruiser was half-buried. The landscape was smoothed, remade. The Eye was near. He could feel it—not just a direction, but a pull.

Jack stood, testing his legs, then looked east—toward the unseen centre of the desert.

Tomorrow, he would reach the Eye.

But already, Jack felt something watching.

And the real journey hadn't even begun.

By morning, the desert lay still, as if exhausted by its own violence. The sky was clear again—too clear, Jack thought, as though the storm had scrubbed even the colour from it. The wind had dropped to nothing, and in its place there was a silence that pressed in on the ears like deep water.

He dug the Land Cruiser out of its bed of sand. He worked wordlessly, his movements methodical, patient. His hands blistered and raw beneath his gloves.

He set off again just after sunrise, the wheels crunching over a terrain now unfamiliar, reshaped overnight. Jack studied the horizon. The landscape had subtly changed—less red, more grey-blue, with curved formations and low ridges like ripples in stone. And then, he crested a rise and he saw it.

The Eye.

The Richat Structure.

It stretched across the earth like the fingerprint of a god— concentric circles of rock and sediment, vast and surreal, as if someone had pressed a thumb into the world and left a mark. From the ground, you couldn't see the full spiral, but the curves were there, undeniable, etched into the terrain like ancient scars.

Jack stepped out of the vehicle and just stood. The heat shimmered around him, but he felt cold. Not fear—something else. Recognition.

Jack moved down the slope, drawn inward, boots crunching over rocks and salt. He felt dizzy. The air grew heavier with each step, not from heat—but from memory, or something like it.

He didn't know what he was looking for until he found it.

Near the centre of the outermost ring, half-buried in dust, was a small collection of stones—not natural. Arranged deliberately. A cairn. Old, maybe decades old. Maybe older.

Jack knelt beside it and brushed away sand with trembling hands. Beneath the top stones, a strip of faded cloth was tied around a rusted tin box. He hesitated, then opened it.

Inside was a photograph, sun-bleached nearly white. Two men, side by side, are seated on a sand dune. One was dark-skinned, wearing traditional robes, smiling broadly. The other—paler, worn—was younger than Jack expected, though the face was strikingly familiar.

He turned the photo over.

Written in faded ink:

"To those who remember"

Jack froze, not from the words, but from the second wall of sand approaching.

He didn't notice due to his attention being focused on 'The Eye'.

This was much bigger, much more fierce than the first. Jack knew then that, as well as being in the Eye of the Sahara, he was also ironically in the eye of the storm and this time it wasn't going to be as forgiving. Jack humorously grabbed Lauren's umbrella and braced for the mother of all sandstorms. Jack wasn't confident he would survive this one. And then it hit and everything went dark.

There was no up. No forward. No past.

The storm lasted not hours — but days, or something that felt like it. He couldn't sleep. Couldn't open his eyes. Couldn't eat.

He drank sand.

He hallucinated.

He saw oceans. Snow. Heard jazz music and his father's voice calling for dinner.

He saw a figure, once, tall, wrapped in red, standing inside the spiral, watching him.

It didn't speak.

It just waited.

At some point, the wind tore the umbrella halfway open — and still he held it, its fabric flapping like a broken sail, ribs bent like bone. But it worked. It held.

When the storm finally died, it didn't go quietly.

It collapsed.

The wind didn't fade. It fell, like a tent folding onto itself.

And then — light.

The sky returned.

Blue. Real.

Jack peeled himself up from the ground.

He was coated in dust, with cracked lips and blood on his knuckles from gripping the umbrella too tightly. His throat rasped when he breathed.

But he stood.

And he was alone, standing in the centre of a perfect spiral — stone, ancient, untouched.

He looked around.

No vehicle. No footprints.

Not even his own.

The umbrella flapped weakly in his hand — a ruin.

He laughed, once. A strange, croaking sound.

Then he started walking — not away, not toward.

Just forward.

Jack awakens half-buried in sand, disoriented. His mouth is full of grit, skin blistering, gear missing. The landscape around him is colourless, blisteringly hot, and silent.

The sand was in his teeth.

Jack doubled over in a fit of coughing, the dry, hacking sound tearing through the silence. His throat burned raw. He turned onto his side, spitting up a bitter mix of sand and bile onto the scorched ground. The dust was everywhere, ground into his clothes, lodged in his ears, stinging behind his eyes. Even under his fingernails, the grit was packed in tight, as if the desert itself had taken hold of him.

He sat up slowly. The world wobbled.

Nothing moved. Nothing made a sound.

The desert rolled away in every direction, a landscape so vast and bare it made the inside of his skull feel hollow. There were no trees, no buildings, no tire tracks—just pale dunes that looked sun-bleached and dead. No truck, nothing familiar, no body, nothing.

He touched his shirt pocket—empty. His phone. Then his pants were still damp with sweat. He patted around. The small leather bag he'd carried—missing. His water bottle lay ten feet away, half buried. He crawled to it. Shook it. A mocking rattle of nothing.

The heat was already tightening around him like a screw.

Jack stood, unsteady. The soles of his boots were cracked and sandy. He turned a slow, stunned circle, one hand shielding his eyes from the angry white sky. The wind had died. Now, only silence remained.

He rubbed his face with both hands and tasted salt and grit. Then he let out a weak laugh. "Brilliant."

The laughter dried up as soon as it began.

He had to move. That much he knew. Just pick a direction and walk. Standing here would bake him. He turned toward what he thought was west and began walking, each step a crunch of sand under dead air.

There was nothing else to do.

*****

He hadn't gone twenty steps when he stopped and yanked his shirt collar open. His chest was red and streaked with sunburn under the linen. He squinted down at his watch.

The face was opaque with dust. He wiped it with the inside of his sleeve. Still blank. He gave it a firm slap.

Nothing.

He pulled the dead phone from his back pocket and wiped it too. The screen flickered once and then died completely. No signal. No time. No maps.

The frustration bubbled up fast.

"Useless bloody thing," he muttered, chucking the phone at the sand. It landed with a sad thud. He didn't bother picking it up.

Next came the water bottle. The plastic was brittle from the sun, and when he opened it, the cap cracked and snapped off in his hand. There was a single mouthful inside. He drank it slowly, trying not to gag on the taste of heated plastic.

He tilted the bottle to catch every drop, then crushed it flat and shoved it back in his pocket.

No landmarks, no compass, no shade.

He turned in another circle, slower this time. The sand had drifted during the storm, erasing any trace of where he had come from. The line of dunes rippled endlessly in every direction, each looking identical to the next. He tried to recall that old woman's voice, something about "follow the shadow of the tallest dune," but that meant nothing now. There were hundreds of tall dunes. And no shadows.

He picked a line of footprints—his own, he assumed—and turned slightly right of them. South? East?

Did it matter?

He walked. Slowly. Deliberately. Trying to breathe through his nose, not his mouth. Every few paces, he paused to listen, but there was no engine, no voices, no wind. Just the occasional click of a shifting dune behind him.

He tried not to think about how far the desert stretched. Or how long the sun would burn. Or how many hours could you live without water?

He focused on walking.

Just keep walking.

He no longer had any sense of time. The sun hung in the same angry spot no matter how far he walked. Each step set his legs ablaze, the muscles in his calves trembling as he forced himself up yet another slope. The sand resisted him—soft and treacherous underfoot, swallowing every ounce of effort as though mocking his progress.

He crested yet another dune and collapsed to his knees at the top, panting like a dog. His tongue stuck to the roof of his mouth.

When he raised his head, he saw it.

A black dot on the next dune over. Unmoving. Alone.

His first instinct was to blink it away, chalk it up to a trick of the heat—the same way the sand shimmered like water in the distance.

But the dot stayed there. A silhouette. Upright. Human.

He stared at it. It didn't move.

His heart kicked.

He stood, swaying. "Hey!" he called.

The figure did not respond.

Jack waved both arms. "HEY!"

Still no response.

He started walking again, half-tumbling down the slope and dragging himself up the next one, eyes fixed on the figure. As he neared, the shape resolved: a man, sitting cross-legged at the peak, back straight, head covered by a long cloth that trailed down his back.

He wore sandals. His hands rested calmly on his knees.

Jack stopped ten feet away, breathing like he'd run a marathon. The man turned his head slowly to look at him.

Dark eyes. Young face. Calm.

Not a mirage.

Jack bent forward, bracing himself on his knees. "Are you real?" he managed.

The man said nothing.

Jack laughed, weakly. "Christ. I've lost it."

The man raised one eyebrow. "English?"

His accent was soft, lilting. Not Mauritanian. Something west of here.

Jack blinked. "Yes. English."

The man nodded once. "Sit."

It wasn't a question. It was said like a doctor giving instructions.

Jack hesitated, then dropped into the sand across from him. The heat from the dune rose up through his clothes.

The man reached into the folds of his robe and pulled out a crust of bread, broken and hardened by the sun. He held it out without speaking.

Jack stared at it.

The man offered it again, more insistently. "You take. Eat slow."

Jack took it with both hands. The crust cracked as he bit into it.

They sat in silence, the desert all around them. No one else in sight.

After a long moment, the man said simply, "Augustus."

Jack nodded. "Jack."

They try to communicate in broken French, English, and Wolof. The man (Augustus) smiles but stays still. Eventually, he offers Jack a piece of hard bread and a gesture: sit.

Augustus studied him the way one might study a lizard—curious, a little amused, not overly concerned.

Jack chewed the bread carefully. It was like biting a rock, but it slowed his panic. He glanced up.

"You're… Gambian?" he guessed, watching Augustus's eyes.

Augustus pointed at his own chest. "Gambia." Then, after a pause, "Banjul."

Jack nodded, although it meant little to him. "What the hell are you doing out here?"

Augustus smiled. Not mockingly—more like someone who'd heard the same question a dozen times and still found it funny.

He said, "Walking."

"Walking?" Jack wiped his mouth. "Christ. You too, huh?"

Augustus made a vague gesture toward the east. "Zouérat," he said, then traced a path with his finger across the air, "Nouadhibou."

Jack frowned. "Train?"

Augustus's smile deepened. He pointed west.

Jack stared into the dunes. "You think there's a train that way?"

Augustus shrugged, but with a certain certainty. "Big train. Ore.. Many kilometres. Maybe today. Maybe tomorrow."

Jack listened; he enjoyed his accent. To any Englishman, it's one of the stereotypical deep African Man's accents that you could imagine. Calm and wise, un-threatening.

Jack squinted. "We'll die waiting."

Augustus tilted his head. "Or walking."

There was a beat of silence between them—hot wind curling around the lip of the dune.

Then Augustus reached again into his robe and withdrew a dirty plastic bottle, its sides warped from heat. He unscrewed the cap and handed it to Jack.

Inside was water—cloudy, but real.

Jack looked at it as if it were gold. "You sure?"

Augustus nodded once. "Half."

Jack drank one cautious mouthful, then another. He capped it and handed it back, unsure how to say thank you.

He settled for: "Abaraka?"

Augustus grinned. "Mandinka bad."

Jack smirked. "Same."

They sat in silence again.

Two specks in an endless sea of sand.

Jack hesitates, then nods. They sit in silence, broken only by the whisper of the wind. The desert stretches out endlessly around them. Jack realises this man might be his only hope.

The wind was starting to pick up again—not a storm, just a steady hiss, like the whisper of a giant moving far below the sand.

Augustus adjusted his turban with practised fingers, wrapping it tighter around his ears. He didn't seem to notice the heat, or the silence, or the sheer scale of emptiness around them. He looked like a man waiting for a bus, not one stranded a hundred miles from civilisation.

Jack scratched his ankle, trying to dislodge sand from his sock. "You been out here long?"

Augustus looked up to the sun. "Many days."

Jack blinked. "Jesus. And you're just… sitting?"

Augustus nodded toward the west. "Waiting. The train will come."

Jack glanced again at the horizon—nothing but shimmer. "You really think so?"

Augustus gave the faintest shrug. "I don't think. I hope."

Jack chewed the inside of his cheek. The kind of answer he hated. No plan, no schedule. Just hope.

He looked back the way he came. No footprints anymore. No way back.

With a groan, he lay back in the sand beside Augustus, one arm draped over his eyes. The sun bit into his exposed wrist. He let it.

The wind curled across the dune again.

Augustus shifted slightly, unwrapping a thin cloth and laying it over both their feet. A quiet gesture. Not a word said.

For the first time since waking, Jack didn't feel like he was already dead.

He didn't trust the man beside him. He didn't understand him. But he wasn't alone anymore.

That would have to do.

Jack woke with sand in his ears and ice in his bones.

The sky was a pale gray dome, not yet lit by the sun but already promising heat. His back ached, neck stiff, lips raw. He coughed and spat dryly. Every breath was scratched on the way down.

Augustus sat a few feet away, facing east, his silhouette still as a monument. His shoes were off. A rectangle of cloth had been spread in front of him. He bent forward, then upright again, whispering quietly.

Jack squinted. "Is that praying?"

Augustus didn't answer.

Jack rubbed his eyes. "Right. Of course it is."

He sat up slowly. His shirt stuck to his back. The skin on his shoulders felt tight—burned, no doubt. He tipped out his boot. Sand spilled like powder, clinging to his socks in fine, stubborn layers, as if it had grown there overnight.

Augustus finished his prayer, folded the cloth with precise care, and slipped it into a side pocket of his robe. Then he stood, looked down at Jack, and said simply, "Time."

Jack blinked. "Time for what?"

"Walk."

Jack let out a brittle laugh. "Where? You got a bloody GPS, I don't know about?"

Augustus ignored him, pulled the cloth tighter over his head, and started down the dune.

Jack stared after him, shaking his head. "Jesus wept," he muttered.

Still, he stood. Still, he followed.

Because in all directions, the sand looked the same—but Augustus at least was moving.

Chapter 2

Sand in the Lungs

The sun was up fully now—too high, too fast. The sand threw off a brutal glare that forced Jack to squint with each step. The sweat had already soaked through his shirt, and they hadn't been walking for half an hour.

Augustus moved with ease, like a man certain his legs would not fail him. His sandals slapped softly against the sand, and the cloth over his head fluttered slightly in the breeze. He stopped abruptly atop a ridge and crouched.

Jack caught up, panting. "Please tell me that's not another rock you want to examine."

Augustus pulled something from the folds of his robe—a small, rusted compass. The glass face was cracked, but the needle inside spun slowly, then quivered to a halt.

He tapped the edge gently and pointed west.

"There," he said. "We go."

Jack stared at the compass. "And you're trusting that thing?"

"It moves," Augustus said, as though that settled it.

"That doesn't mean it's right."

"It is better than nothing."

Jack sighed. "How do we even know the train runs out here? What if we're too far south?"

Augustus didn't look at him. "We are not."

Jack pressed. "You sure? Because we could walk in the wrong direction and die just as fast."

Augustus turned his head slowly. "Everything is wrong direction if you stop."

Jack scoffed. "That's fortune-cookie logic."

Augustus smiled faintly. "I don't know this cookie."

Jack knelt in the sand, breathing hard. "We need to find a road. A radio tower. Something that leads to people."

Augustus pointed again. "Train has people."

"Train has ore."

Augustus stood. "Ore needs people."

Jack gritted his teeth. "What if it doesn't come?"

Augustus shrugged. "Then we see something else."

Jack looked at him for a long moment. "You're insane."

Augustus started walking.

"Wait—wait, just…" Jack got up. "Fine. Fine."

He followed again.

Not because he believed. Because Augustus had a direction.

And direction, right now, was enough.

The wind picked up again by midmorning, curling around their ankles and sending little flurries of sand across their path. Each gust erased their footprints almost as soon as they made them.

They came upon it unexpectedly—just over the crest of a long slope.

Jack was the first to see the curve of bones.

He stopped, blinking. "Jesus…"

A camel, or what was left of one. Its bones were picked clean, bleached a ghostly white. Ribs arched upward in a wide cage, half-buried, curved like frozen fingers grasping at the air. The skull was cracked clean down the centre.

Augustus walked over without a word and crouched beside it.

"Poor bastard," Jack murmured, wiping sweat from his brow.

Augustus didn't answer. He had spotted something wedged between the exposed spine and a clump of dune grass—a canvas satchel, faded blue. He reached in carefully and pulled it free.

Jack watched as Augustus opened the flap.

Inside: a few shrivelled dates, two broken nuts, a rust-speckled shard of mirror, and a photograph. Augustus handed it to him.

A child. Five or six, maybe. Big eyes, tight braids. Smiling. Torn at the corner.

Jack swallowed. "Someone had plans."

Augustus nodded slowly.

He took the photo back, looked at it one more time, then slid it into the satchel and stood.

"What are you going to do with that?" Jack asked.

"Leave it," Augustus said. "Too late for him. Not too late for us."

Jack glanced back at the bones. The ribs caught the light like delicate porcelain.

He looked away.

They kept walking.

The light was beginning to distort.

Each step brought fresh flickers at the edge of Jack's vision—shapes that didn't stay put, shadows that twitched and vanished the moment he turned toward them. The sting of salt pricked his skin. Was he crying? Sweating? Both?

He stumbled once, caught himself on a slope, and kept walking, jaw clenched.

The horizon ahead wavered. He squinted hard.

There. A structure.

Rectangular. Metal. Like a water tank on stilts. A tall pole beside it—no, a flag. A green flag. It was flapping.

He shaded his eyes. "Augustus."

Augustus kept walking.

Jack grabbed his arm. "Augustus. There's something there."

Augustus followed his gaze. Looked. Waited.

Then turned back to him, face unreadable. "What colour flag?"

"Green."

Augustus sighed softly. "Again green."

"What do you mean by 'again'? That's a tank, I can see—"

Augustus stepped forward, raised one hand, and slapped Jack gently across the cheek.

Not hard. But sharp enough.

Jack reeled back, blinking. "What the hell, man—!"

Augustus pointed to the mirage. "Watch."

Jack turned.

The flag was gone.

The tank blurred at the edges. Then flickered. And then—

Gone.

Only air and heat.

Jack's knees buckled slightly. "Jesus…"

He stared at the empty horizon. His throat was closing up again, his skin crawling.

"I heard someone," he whispered. "A voice. A woman."

Augustus looked at him calmly. "Third mirage today."

Jack turned to him, furious. "You knew it wasn't real. Why didn't you say something?"

"You needed to see."

"For what? A laugh?"

Augustus shook his head. "Now you believe the sun can lie."

Jack didn't respond. He just stood there, trembling, watching the nothingness.

Augustus walked on.

Eventually, Jack followed.

The sun was dropping fast now, a red-hot coin pressed low against the horizon. The dunes caught the light in long, slanting shadows, and the temperature had begun its daily collapse. The heat didn't leave—it receded, like something crouching just out of reach.

Jack was limping, his right foot blistered raw. Every joint in his body ached. His tongue felt thick and dry in his mouth, and his vision had narrowed to a tunnel ahead of him—Augustus's back, moving steadily forward, always forward.

He couldn't do this much longer.

He muttered, "I'm done."

Augustus kept walking.

Jack sank to one knee, panting. "Augustus. I'm serious."

Augustus stopped. His head tilted, not toward Jack, but to the west. Then he turned slowly, silently, and pointed.

Jack looked.

At first, he saw nothing.

Then—there. A line.

A thin, straight line cutting across the base of the horizon. It didn't ripple like the dunes. It didn't curve. It didn't move.

Jack narrowed his eyes. "That's…"

Augustus said nothing.

Jack took a few shaky steps forward, trying to get a clearer view.

The line was still there. Too even, too deliberate. It ran horizontally, stretching on for what felt like an eternity.

"Train?" Jack breathed.

Augustus nodded once.

"Or mirage?"

Augustus didn't answer.

Jack stared. His breath slowed.

That line was either salvation—or the cruellest illusion yet.

But something deep inside him said: It's real.

This time, it's real.

Chapter 3

Iron Dust

The line sharpened as they drew closer—too straight, too black to be anything natural. It ran like a scar through the landscape, cutting across the beige dunes with impossible certainty.

Jack felt his breath catching again, not from exhaustion this time, but disbelief. "It's real," he muttered. "Bloody hell, it's actually real."

Augustus said nothing, just kept walking.

Soon, the sand turned darker, coarser underfoot. Flecks of rusted brown began to appear, and then they stepped onto it: the rail bed, raised just slightly, lined with crushed rock and iron flakes that crunched beneath their boots.

The tracks shimmered under the heat like wet snakes.

Jack crouched, pressed two fingers to the steel. It was warm. Not hot. But recently touched by the sun—or something else.

Augustus walked ahead, eyes scanning the length of the line. One direction stretched forever into the desert; the other vanished over the horizon behind a slight bend. No signs of life. No noise. Just wind.

Iron dust swirled in slow, lazy spirals around them.

Jack stood and shaded his eyes. "This is the one, yeah? The mining train?"

Augustus nodded.

"Goes all the way to the Atlantic?"

"Nouadhibou," Augustus confirmed. "Longest train."

"How long?"

Augustus shrugged. "Too long to count."

Jack exhaled. "And we're supposed to just—what? Wave it down?"

Augustus tilted his head. "We get on."

Jack looked at the tracks again. "There's no passenger car."

Augustus tapped his chest. "Passengers make car."

Jack laughed, sharp and tired. "Wonderful."

They stood there a while longer, just two figures swallowed by the edge of the world.

Then Augustus knelt, laid his ear gently against the steel.

He didn't move.

Jack watched, uncertain whether to feel comforted or worried.

The silence was total—until the faintest murmur seemed to rise from the far end of the rail.

The tracks stretched into infinity, twin black veins slicing the desert. The further they walked, the stranger the dust became—thicker, redder, coating their shoes, then their ankles, until every step left a rust-colored ghost behind them.

Augustus kept close to the rail, head bowed, eyes keen, moving with the patience of a man well accustomed to waiting. Jack followed a little behind, now limping, his blistered foot throbbing in protest.

"Are we sure it comes this way?" he asked for the third time.

Augustus didn't look up. "Yes."

"How often?"

"Sometimes once," Augustus said. "Sometimes two."

"Two what? Times? Days?"

Augustus only shrugged.

Jack swore under his breath. "Brilliant. It could be ten minutes. Could be next week."

Augustus stopped walking and turned. "You want to stop? Stop."

Jack wiped his face. "No. I want a plan."

Augustus stepped off the track and crouched. He pressed his ear to the rail again, waited, then shook his head.

Jack watched him, arms crossed. "What do you hear?"

"Nothing yet. Wait….I hear…. Englishman being impatient"

"Oh, very funny! Then maybe we should rest. Just for a minute."

Augustus looked at the sky. Then at Jack. Then sat, slowly. "One minute."

Jack dropped beside him with a grunt. The gravel dug into his back.

They sat in silence, broken only by the faint whisper of wind and the occasional ticking sound of heat escaping metal.

Jack looked up at the sky. Pale blue, scattered with long, dirty streaks of cloud. The kind of sky that never promised rain.

"You ever been on it?" he asked.

Augustus shook his head. "Seen it. Never rode."

Jack nodded slowly. "We get on… what then?"

Augustus smiled faintly. "Then we don't die in sand."

It wasn't the answer Jack wanted. But it was the only one that mattered.

He closed his eyes just for a moment.

Then Augustus's voice came sharp: "Listen."

Jack blinked, sat up.

Far down the track—barely audible at first—there it was.

A low, steady growl. Mechanical. Relentless. Growing.

Augustus stood.

"The train," he said.

The sound deepened as it grew closer—not a roar, not yet, but a low, endless drone, like something ancient turning in its sleep. A slow exhale of iron and fire from the bones of the desert itself.

Augustus stepped back from the rails and narrowed his eyes. "Soon."

Jack stood, adrenaline breaking over his exhaustion like a wave. "Where? I don't—"

Augustus pointed.

And then Jack saw it too.

Far down the line, a dense wall of red dust billowed upward, as though the desert had suddenly decided to breathe. At the centre of it, a black mass slowly emerged—rectangular shapes chained together, stretching impossibly far in both directions.

Jack blinked. "That's… Christ."

It wasn't just long—it was endless. The train devoured the horizon. Hundreds of ore cars, each one open-topped and piled high with black-red rock. No windows, no doors, no ladders. Just rusted metal and raw minerals.

"Is it slowing?" Jack asked, uncertain.

"No," Augustus said. "Not here."

"So how the hell do we—"

"Run."

"What?"

"When close, we run."

Jack stared at him. "We're supposed to jump onto that?"

Augustus turned to him calmly. "We miss, we die. So we don't miss."

The train was closing fast now, its sound changing—rising into a thunder that made the rocks underfoot tremble.

Jack's mouth went dry. His legs felt like sandbags.

Augustus didn't move. He was scanning the cars, judging speed, spacing, angles. His expression sharpened.

"Next hill," he said, pointing. "Easier. We go there."

Jack followed, stumbling as he ran. They moved up a short embankment of loose gravel, dust choking their throats. The train was louder now—screaming metal on metal. Ore dust swirled around them like red smoke.

The lead engine thundered past, then the first cars—dozens of them, all alike, all high-walled and filled to the brim.

"Wait," Augustus said. "Wait…"

Jack crouched, hands on his knees, heart pounding like a jackhammer.

Augustus's eyes flicked from car to car.

Then he said one word:

"Now."

The train screamed past, wind and ore-dust hammering them in the face.

Augustus ran first, feet sure on the uneven slope beside the track, eyes locked on a particular car—a half-loaded one, lower than the others, its edges caked with rust and streaks of reddish-black grime.

Jack chased after him, slipping twice on the loose gravel, one shoe almost flying off. The noise was deafening, metal wheels shrieking, ore grinding, the engine's bellow—filling his skull, his chest, his whole world.

"Go!" Augustus shouted.

He veered closer, reached out, caught the iron lip of the ore car's side with both hands, and vaulted—his feet scrambling on the outer plate before disappearing over the edge.

Jack pushed himself harder. His legs weren't obeying. His breath came in shudders. He reached the same car five seconds later—but the angle was wrong. The car was already past.

He jumped anyway.

His hands slapped against metal. Slid.

His left foot hit the base and bounced off. The car dragged past. He lost grip.

His knees hit gravel, tearing open. He cried out, one hand still on the rim.

Then Augustus's arm appeared—reaching down from above.

"Take!"

Jack grabbed for him. Missed.

Augustus reached lower, nearly falling out of the car himself. "Now!"

Jack leapt up with everything he had and caught Augustus's forearm.

A jolt of pain shot through his shoulder, but he held on. Augustus grunted, pulled—slowly, painfully—and Jack scraped and clawed his way up and over the rim.

They both collapsed into the ore with heavy thuds, coughing, gasping, coated in iron dust.

The train thundered on.

They lie in an open ore car, panting and bleeding. Iron dust coats everything. The noise of the train is deafening. But they've made it for now.

The ore felt like shattered glass.

Jack lay on his back, panting in broken gasps, his body half-submerged in the jagged black rocks. Each breath sucked in red dust, every inhale scraped down his throat like dry grit. His fingers were bleeding. His knees stung raw.

But he was alive.

Beside him, Augustus lay on his side, one hand gripping the rim of the car, the other clutching his ribs. His eyes were shut, chest rising and falling like a piston.

Neither of them spoke for a while. They didn't need to.

The train screamed around them, a steel monster with no regard for its passengers. The noise was relentless—a constant, thundering vibration that swallowed thought. It vibrated in their teeth, in their spines.

Jack turned his head slowly. The car they were in was half-full, the iron ore sharp-edged and uneven. The rim came up to his shoulders when he sat. No roof. No shade. Just sky.

He spat, tried to wipe the dust from his face, and gave up.

Augustus opened one eye. "You are heavy," he said, his voice thin.

Jack let out a short, cracked laugh. "You're a lunatic."

They didn't smile. There was no energy for smiling.

Only the train, the heat, and the sound of a thousand tons of iron hurtling west.

They lay still, letting the desert recede behind them.

The train didn't slow down.

It screamed forward without apology, churning up dust and rust in its wake. The iron ore car bucked and jolted beneath them like a living thing. The floor was just sharp-edged rock and steel—no cushion, no comfort.

Jack sat with his knees drawn to his chest, his head swathed in his shirt. Only his eyes peeked out, squinting against the sun and grit. His skin felt crusted with salt, his breathing shallow.

Augustus had fashioned a crude turban from a strip of his robe and tied a rag over his mouth. His posture remained steady, but his eyes were red and his lips cracked.

Hours passed like that. The sky shifted from a hard white to gold.

Occasionally, they glimpsed other cars—some empty, some holding cargo that looked like bundled wire or metal drums. Once, Jack thought he saw a goat in one car, but it vanished in the haze.

And then he noticed the shape.

Two cars ahead, diagonally across the line of movement. A figure.

It wasn't lying flat or hiding—it was upright, sitting on the mound of ore like a statue. Legs folded. Head tilted just slightly downward, facing them.

Watching.

Jack nudged Augustus.

He pointed.

Augustus followed his gaze and stiffened.

The man didn't move.

Jack raised a hand and waved once.

Nothing.

"He's just… sitting there," Jack said.

Augustus didn't reply.

The figure stayed perfectly still, even as the wind tore at his robe. His face was obscured by shadow and cloth. He seemed immune to the shaking of the train, to the heat, to the dust.

Like he belonged there.

Like he'd always been there.

Chapter 4

The Man in the Car

The man hadn't moved.

Even as the train rounded a long, slow curve and the shadows stretched across the dunes, he remained in the same posture—legs crossed, hands in his lap, head cocked just enough to suggest attention.

Not sleeping. Not rest.

Observation.

Jack watched him carefully. Every time he blinked, he expected the man to vanish—just another sun trick. But he didn't.

"What do you think?" Jack asked.

Augustus said nothing.

Jack turned. "Augustus?"

He was staring at the man now, too, but with a different expression—tight, unreadable.

"I don't like," he muttered.

"Why?"

"No food. No water. No cover." He looked at Jack. "No blink."

Jack exhaled. "He's probably just mad."

"Maybe."

"Or maybe he's got it figured out."

Augustus's jaw tensed. "Maybe he's not real."

45

Jack glanced again. The man was still watching.

"Do you recognise him?" he asked.

Augustus shook his head. "Too far. Too still."

The train clattered beneath them, a rhythm of metal and dust and grinding steel.

Jack shifted uncomfortably. "We should talk to him."

Augustus didn't respond.

"I mean, what if he has something? Water? Info?"

Still nothing.

Jack gestured vaguely. "You're the one who said people ride this train. Well, he's people. Sort of."

Augustus finally said, "Some people are better off."

The man's robes fluttered in the wind, but he remained as he was—silent, still, unmoved by time or motion.

A shape out of place.

Or maybe exactly in place.

The light was fading now, bleeding gold and blood-orange across the top of the desert. The wind had changed—stronger, colder, laden with grit. It sliced through their clothing and whistled through the gaps between cars, high and shrill.

Jack hunched down lower. "It's going to be freezing tonight."

Augustus was staring at the watching man.

Jack noticed the shift in his body—slight forward lean, a tightening in his legs. "Don't even think about it," he said.

Augustus stood.

"Augustus."

"We look. We ask. Then we go."

Jack grabbed his arm. "What if he's armed? What if he pushes us off?"

Augustus didn't answer. He adjusted his headwrap, climbed to the edge of their car, and dropped down between it and the next.

"Unbelievable," Jack muttered.

He watched Augustus cross the first link—nothing more than two slabs of iron, narrow and vibrating. Below, the tracks flashed past in a blur of white and black and red. A single wrong step would end things quickly and without ceremony.

Augustus moved slowly, hands out for balance.

Jack hesitated, then cursed under his breath and followed.

The moment his feet hit the narrow steel connector, the vibration struck him—up through his boots, into his knees, his spine. The air whipped around him. He clung to the lip of the next ore car, heart hammering.

They crossed again.

And again.

Each car required a leap, a pull upward, a moment of total exposure.

Finally, they reached the edge of the car where the man sat.

Still unmoving.

Still watching.

Augustus turned and looked at Jack.

Jack gave the smallest nod.

Then they climbed up into the man's car.

At first, he seemed nothing more than a heap of discarded cloth—robes bleached pale by the sun, turban wrapped too many times to count. Only his eyes were visible, dry and yellowish, slightly sunken in.

He sat atop the ore as if the moving train were a prayer mat. His posture was flawless. Balanced. Timeless.

Augustus and Jack pulled themselves up onto the edge of the car and paused.

The man didn't react. Didn't flinch. Didn't even blink.

Jack cleared his throat. "Bonsoir."

Nothing.

Augustus took a cautious step forward. "As-salamu alaykum."

The man's head turned, slow as rusted hinges.

He looked at Jack.

"W'alaykum," he said, voice sandpaper-thin.

A long pause.

"You ride too," he said. French-accented, but strange. Words clipped.

Jack crouched nearby. "Just started. We barely made it."

Initially puzzled, the man paused and then nodded, as if this explained something. "The train eats many. You are lucky. Or unlucky."

Jack's brow furrowed. "How long have you been on it?"

The man tilted his head, his eyes narrowing. "How long is not right. The better word is how deep."

Jack raised an eyebrow. "You been drinking the iron?"

The man smiled, faintly. It didn't reach his eyes.

"My name is M'barek," he said. "Or it was. Names are soft things. They fall away."

Jack shifted uneasily. "You work with the train?"

M'barek looked past him, toward the dunes. "The train works with no one. It moves because the desert moves. It goes because the wind remembers."

Jack frowned. "Right. Okay."

M'barek tapped the ore with one finger. "It always runs from the red hole to the black sea. Some say it has no driver. Others say it is a punishment."

Jack scoffed. "A punishment?"

M'barek's gaze sharpened. "Everything in this land is either punishment or waiting."

The wind screamed across the top of the car.

Augustus shifted his footing. "We go back."

M'barek said softly, "You should not stay here tonight."

Jack looked at Augustus.

"Why not?" he asked.

M'barek's eyes didn't blink. "Because the ones who got off too late ride between the cars. And they don't like the living."

Augustus turned. "We go."

Jack hesitated.

M'barek smiled again. "They never believe the first time."

The sun had almost vanished, leaving only a smear of blood-orange on the horizon. The temperature was falling fast, the kind of sudden drop that made joints ache and breath sting.

M'barek hadn't moved.

He sat perfectly still on his little throne of ore, his robe flapping slightly in the evening wind. His eyes, though dim and aged, stayed sharp—tracking something just beyond the edge of night.

Augustus was already halfway to the edge of the car, gripping the side to begin the crossing back.

Jack lingered a moment longer.

"You keep saying we shouldn't stay here," he said. "Why?"

M'barek didn't look at him. "Because when the heat dies, the doors open."

"What doors?"

M'barek raised a single, gloved finger and pointed—not toward any visible thing, but downwards, into the narrow black gulf between the cars, the darkness stretching between each massive coupling.

"There."

Jack followed his gaze.

All he saw was air. Steel. Darkness between moving cars.

Then M'barek added, almost gently, "They ride there. The ones who got off too late. You stay, you'll see."

Jack glanced back at Augustus. He was already looking back, tense.

Jack lowered his voice. "You mean ghosts?"

M'barek didn't respond right away. Then:

"I mean memory with teeth."

That did it.

Jack stepped back.

M'barek turned slightly, one hand lifting in a vague gesture of farewell—or warning.

"Sleep near the middle," he said. "They don't like iron that sings."

Augustus's voice cut in sharply. "Jack."

Jack turned and climbed down.

The two of them crossed back as the light died completely, the wind tearing louder through the metal gaps, making it impossible not to glance down as they passed.

Nothing there.

But Jack didn't look too long.

Chapter 5

Offloading

The train's rhythm changed.

It was subtle at first—less clatter, more groan. The pitch of the wheels dipped. The air around them felt… different.

Augustus lifted his head, listening. "Slowing."

Jack blinked grit from his eyes. "Is that good or bad?"

Augustus didn't answer. He crawled to the edge of the car and peered over.

Jack followed, shielding his face from the wind. Ahead, in the dusky light, the outlines of a settlement appeared—if it could be called that. A wide slab of concrete split the tracks like a scar. One rusted shack leaned against a water tank, and two others squatted beside it, roofless and half-collapsed. Beyond them, a row of low stone walls and scraps of fencing marked what might once have been an enclosure.

No signs, no flags. But there were men.

Two of them stood near the shack, rifles slung lazily over their shoulders. They smoked and muttered in Hassaniya, one occasionally spitting into the dust. Their posture said boredom, not vigilance.

Further off, a generator coughed to life.

The train shuddered again—then eased into a near stop. The wheels hissed but didn't lock. The movement was like a breathing beast, reluctant to rest.

Jack ducked lower. "Why are we stopping here?"

Augustus whispered, "Checkpoint. Maybe fuel. Maybe bribe."

"You think they'll check the cars?"

Augustus shook his head. "Not tonight. Not all."

From a nearby car came a muffled shout, followed by laughter.

Then boots on gravel. Workers, or guards, are moving along the line. Somewhere, a woman called out in Arabic. Another voice answered with a slurred mix of French and something else.

The night had fallen, but the heat still clung to the metal. In the half-light, the scene below looked ghostly—pale buildings, slow shapes, long shadows.

Jack turned to Augustus. "We're getting off, aren't we?"

Augustus's face was unreadable.

Then: "A little."

The wind had eased, but the air was heavy with iron and diesel.

Augustus went first, as always. He swung over the rim of the ore car, hung for a heartbeat, then dropped. His sandals met the gravel with barely a sound. He glanced up, a quick gesture urging Jack to follow.

Jack hesitated.

The guards were nowhere in sight now—moved off toward one of the shacks, judging by the murmur of conversation and the occasional clink of a bottle. Farther down the train, someone was lighting a fire in a metal drum.

The whole outpost seemed to be in a kind of sleepwalking state, men drifting like shadows around the train, half-seen, half-real.

Jack swung one leg over the rim and dropped.

His knees buckled slightly on impact, but he kept upright. Augustus handed him a strip of cloth.

"Wrap face," he whispered. "Quiet."

They moved quickly, sticking to the shadows cast by the tall cars. The side of the track was scattered with rusted tools, broken crates, and torn tarps. The desert didn't so much reclaim things here—it simply forgot them.

The water tank loomed ahead, its side dented and streaked with dried runoff. A long rubber hose curled from one end like a dead snake.

Augustus tested the nozzle. Nothing.

He crouched, followed the hose's line to the base, and jimmied open a valve near a metal box. There was a gurgling sound—then a weak stream of water trickled from the hose.

Jack dropped beside him, cupped his hands, and drank.

It tasted like rust and old pipes. But it was cold.

They filled two crushed plastic bottles, stuffing them back into Augustus's robe. Then they turned, fast and low, moving back toward the car.

But the train had shifted.

They didn't make it all the way back to their car.

Just as Augustus dropped down again to double-check the hose, a soft metallic clink echoed from somewhere behind them. Not boots. Something lighter. A pan? A tin?

Jack turned and froze.

A woman stood under the lean-to next to the water tank, half-shadowed by a corrugated iron wall. Her skin was dark, her head wrapped in a scarf patterned with faint red and green. She held a dented metal pot in both hands and stared at them—not alarmed, not smiling. Just watching.

Augustus straightened slowly.

The woman spoke in Hassaniya Arabic—gentle, clipped. Jack didn't understand, but Augustus nodded once, then gestured for him to follow.

Jack whispered, "What'd she say?"

"She says, Come quiet. Not her problem."

"That's reassuring."

She led them behind the tank, through a cracked door into what must have once been a kitchen—long-unused stove, stacks of oil cans, rusted shelves. In the corner sat a metal table with one good leg and three broken ones, supported by rocks.

She set down the pot and from beneath a shelf, drew out a blue plastic jug and a piece of cloth-wrapped bread.

Augustus took them with both hands. "Shukran, ya Hawa."

Jack blinked. "You know her?"

Augustus nodded. "From before. Long time."

Jack sat heavily on an overturned bucket. "You know everyone out here?"

"No. Just the good ones."

The woman—Hawa—moved through the space with quiet efficiency. She neither asked questions nor spared Jack a second glance. She poured water into a small cup and passed it to him as if she had done so a thousand times before.

Her husband appeared a moment later—taller, older, eyes sunken but alert. He stopped when he saw Jack, then looked at Hawa.

Words passed between them—quick, quiet, in Wolof or maybe Pulaar.

Then the man, Moustapha, turned to Jack and said, in thickly accented French, "You leave soon."

Jack nodded. "Oui. Bientôt."

Moustapha stared a moment longer, then stepped outside, pulling the curtain shut.

Augustus leaned toward Jack. "They let us rest. Not more."

Jack took another sip from the cup. "I'll take it."

They sat in silence. Just for a moment, it felt like somewhere else.

Somewhere safer.

The room was lit by a single oil lamp set on an upside-down crate. Its glow barely reached the corners, but it made the dust in the air look golden.

Hawa squatted near the pot, stirring something Jack couldn't see. Augustus sat on a cloth beside her, hunched but relaxed. Jack leaned against the wall, the cool cement grounding his back.

"She's kind to you," Jack said quietly.

Augustus nodded. "She helped me once. Long road."

"What kind of help?"

He shrugged. "Sometimes water is more than water."

Hawa spoke then—slow, soft—and Augustus translated without her needing to ask.

"She says many come through. Mali, Senegal, Niger. Some by bus, some by foot. Some on top of trains."

Jack looked at her. "They're all going to Spain?"

Augustus translated again. Then: "She says not all. Some die before choosing."

Jack rubbed his face. "Charming."

Hawa said something more, her eyes narrowed.

Augustus frowned. "She says after Choum, it is bad."

"Bad how?"

"She says many men ride between cars. Hide in gaps. Take things."

"Like robbers?"

Augustus nodded slowly. "Yes. But hungry ones."

Jack exhaled. "Wonderful."

Hawa stood and went to the curtain, opened it just wide enough to glance outside. When she returned, Moustapha followed her in.

He didn't sit. Just looked at them both and spoke in a stern, low voice. Augustus listened carefully, then relayed:

"He says if you stay too long, someone will sell you."

Jack stared at him.

Augustus gave a weak smile. "He means well."

"What else did he say?"

"That we get back on the train before it moves. Or we stay here, work for food. No free ride."

Jack looked at Hawa, who was watching him again—not coldly, but with distance.

Then at Moustapha, who crossed his arms.

Then, finally, in Augustus. "We go now?"

Augustus stood. "Now."

Offloading

Outside, the wind had shifted again—cooler now, tinged with rust and diesel. The train, which had been resting like a massive, breathing animal, gave a groan. The cars clanked and hissed as if grumbling back to life.

Augustus stepped through the curtain first, checking the shadows. "Go," he said softly.

They moved at a clip, skirting the cracked water tank, the blackened husk of what might once have been a truck. The checkpoint guards lingered in the distance, silhouettes bent to their fire, voices low, heat-hazed and unaware.

The train let out a long, low warning blast.

Augustus broke into a jog. Jack followed, pulse rising, the ore cars looming darker by the minute.

They reached the side of their car and climbed quickly—Augustus first, Jack scrambling after. His hands ached from the earlier climb, and his legs threatened to cramp, but he made it, tumbling down into the same bed of jagged ore.

The vibration had returned.

The train was moving again.

Augustus wiped his hands on his robe. "We stay in the middle now."

Jack nodded, panting. "No more detours."

He looked back toward the outpost—just as a gust of wind parted the dust and light.

There, against the far wall of the shack, stood a figure.

M'barek.

Wrapped in his robes, turban low over his face. Motionless. Watching.

Jack blinked.

Augustus followed his gaze. "You see him?"

Jack swallowed. "Yeah."

Neither of them spoke.

The train pulled away from the outpost, gathering speed.

M'barek didn't wave. Didn't move.

He simply faded back into the dark as the checkpoint disappeared behind them.

Inching forward—almost imperceptibly, but enough to matter.

Augustus jumped first, grabbed a rung and hoisted himself up.

Jack reached for the metal. Missed.

The car began to drift just out of reach.

Augustus leaned out, arm extended. "Jack!"

Jack ran three steps, jumped, caught the lower edge, and scrambled—his foot slipping on gravel—until Augustus caught his wrist and pulled hard.

He tumbled into the ore, breathless, heart slamming.

Augustus grinned. "Like goat."

Jack glared at him. "Next time, I'm sending you for water."

Augustus laughed, quiet and sharp, and they sank back into the dust as the checkpoint faded behind them.

Chapter 6

Walk North

The jolt came without warning.

Jack was drifting—half-asleep, cheek pressed against sun-warmed ore—when the entire car lurched beneath him. He rolled, swore, and caught the edge just before his ribs hit the metal rim.

Augustus was already up, crouched, looking ahead.

This wasn't like the last stop. There were voices. Loud ones.

And vehicles.

Jack pushed himself up onto his knees, blinking away the remnants of sleep and the grit in his eyes. He spotted them at once; dozens of people gathered on a broad, dusty platform, most standing idle. Men in long coats carried radios and rifles. Two military trucks idled beside a low bunker, while a voice bellowed through a megaphone.

"Where are we?" Jack asked.

Augustus's face was tight. "Choum."

The word meant nothing to Jack—but the tone did.

"I thought we were avoiding this place."

"We were," Augustus said. "We didn't."

They stayed low, crouched behind the lip of the car. More figures passed below—soldiers, by the look of them. Their uniforms mismatched, dusty, the kind of gear that looked inherited rather than

63

issued. A group of men walked along the cars, checking inside each one.

Jack ducked lower. "They're searching."

Augustus nodded. "For what?"

"I don't plan to ask."

They both dropped silently over the far side, landing in the gravel and staying low as the boots passed by above. One man leaned into a car behind them and barked something in French. Another laughed. Then came a clatter of metal, a cough, and a smell—cigarette smoke and oil.

Augustus tapped Jack's shoulder. "We go now."

"To where?"

"North."

Jack hesitated. Looked back at the train.

The ore cars stretched behind them—familiar now, almost comforting in their danger. But ahead: too many eyes, too many questions.

He followed Augustus into the dark.

The desert swallowed their footsteps as the train groaned on without them.

The desert was different here.

It was flatter, yes—but not easier. Gone were the high dunes and soft golden waves. This was packed earth, scattered gravel, occasional bursts of low thorn bushes, and flat gray stone that stretched like a dried-up lake. Everything was quiet except for their footfalls and the rasp of breath.

They walked single-file through a dried riverbed, its banks cracked and dotted with old boot prints. Occasionally, they passed a rusted barrel or a plastic bottle crushed into the sand.

Jack kicked one aside. "You think anyone made it this way?"

Augustus shrugged. "Some. Not many."

"What happened to the rest?"

He didn't answer.

They kept walking.

Hours passed. The sun burned the back of Jack's neck through his shirt. Sweat stuck his collar to his skin. He wanted to stop, but the stillness around them was like a dare—if they paused too long, the land might swallow them whole.

Eventually, they reached a cluster of small, sun-bleached stones arranged in a crude circle. A fire pit. Long dead.

Augustus sat. Jack followed, collapsing beside him.

After a while, Augustus spoke. "I left The Gambia five months ago."

Jack looked at him. Augustus was staring out at nothing.

"Boat to Dakar. Then the bus. Then walking. A little money, not much. I gave most to a man who said he had a car. He did not."

Jack wiped sweat from his brow. "Does that happen a lot?"

Augustus nodded. "Many lies. Many smiles."

He reached into his pocket and pulled out a scrap of paper—creased, sun-stained. It had once been a brochure. A photo of a cargo ship, with people waving. The text read CONFIANCE. TRANSPORT À L'EUROPE.

Jack studied it. "You believed this?"

Augustus smiled faintly. "I needed to."

Jack hesitated, then said, "I told my wife I'd go on a short trip. Clear my head."

"Is that why you came?"

"No." Jack looked down at the dust. "I didn't want to go home anymore."

Augustus nodded, slowly, like he understood more than he let on.

"We walk," he said softly, rising again.

Jack stood too, joints stiff. He glanced behind them—no sign of the train, no sign of life.

Just ghost roads, winding toward nothing.

They stumble upon an abandoned white UN Land Cruiser, its frame half-buried in drifting sand. Inside lay a cracked radio, a few dried food packets, two unopened bottles of water, and a seat stained with dried blood. They gathered whatever could be salvaged.

They saw it before they could name it.

Just a glint at first—something metallic beneath the sun. Not a rock, not a mirage. Then the shape began to resolve: a hulk buried nose-down in sand, one rear wheel half-exposed, door flung open like a broken wing.

"A car?" Jack said, squinting.

"Truck," Augustus corrected.

As they neared, the letters became visible through the grime: a faded U and a barely-legible N on the side. A white Land Cruiser. Official. Once.

It sat awkwardly on the slope of a dry wash, the front windshield cracked in a spiderweb, sand piling at the base like snow against a wall. Bullet holes—three, maybe four—decorated the passenger door.

Augustus circled the vehicle cautiously. Jack stood back.

"Anyone inside?"

"No."

They pried open the rear door. The hinges groaned. Inside, it was a tomb.

The cabin reeked of old sweat and rust. Sand had blown in through every crack. The driver's seat was stained dark at the headrest—red, dried, old. Flies buzzed lazily in the footwell.

Augustus reached into the glove box, pulled out a plastic packet—rations, French label. He smelled it. Nodded. Tossed it to Jack.

"Eat slow."

Jack caught it and looked at the label: Repas complet, ration individuelle.

The back seat held a jerry can, half-full. A med kit, mostly empty. Two water bottles rolled under the driver's seat. Augustus handed one over.

"Take both," Jack said. "You need them more."

Augustus shook his head. "We need them same."

Jack looked again at the bloodstain. "What happened here?"

Augustus shrugged. "Same thing that happens everywhere."

He climbed into the passenger seat, opened the glove box again, and pulled out a cracked radio. The antenna was snapped. He turned a dial. Nothing.

Jack reached up and turned it again. A sharp whine of static. Then silence.

Augustus looked at him. "It's dead."

Jack looked out the window. "So's whoever drove this."

They stayed in the shade of the truck a while longer, drinking warm water and eating crackers that tasted like cardboard.

When they left, they didn't look back.

Night came quickly.

One moment, they were walking through a field of black stone, and the next, the sky was ink and the stars ignited, scattered in wild constellations. There was no light but the moon. No sound but the wind against rock and their breath.

They stopped in the lee of a low dune. Augustus gathered a few pieces of brush from a dry creek bed and built a small fire—barely more than a glow, but enough to chase the cold from their hands.

Jack sat with his back against a flat slab of rock, chewing the last of the ration pack, watching the fire flicker in Augustus's eyes.

Augustus said nothing for a long time.

Then: "I lied."

Jack looked up. "About what?"

Augustus stared into the flames. "I told my mother I was going to work. On the coast. Port jobs. Carrying fish. Lifting crates. Nothing special."

Jack stayed quiet.

Augustus's voice dropped lower. "She asked if I would come back. I said yes."

He reached into his shirt and pulled out a small bundle wrapped in plastic—creased, stained. Inside was a photo: a boy, maybe eleven or twelve, standing in front of a tin-roofed house, squinting at the camera, his smile wide.

"My brother," Augustus said. "He thinks I am sending him a phone. And shoes. That was the promise."

Jack took the photo carefully, studied it, then handed it back.

"I had no job," Augustus said. "No port. Only the name of a man in Nouadhibou. I paid to speak to him. That was all."

"You're heading to Spain," Jack said softly.

Augustus nodded. "I was always heading to Spain."

Jack didn't respond for a long time. Then:

"Why tell me now?"

"Because I think we are close. And maybe… it is right to tell it before the sea."

Jack leaned his head back against the stone. "You think your brother's waiting?"

Augustus smiled, sad and sharp. "He is waiting for the man I pretended to be."

Jack looked at the stars. "Then maybe you should become him."

Augustus chuckled softly. "That is also a lie."

They sat in silence, the fire crackling, the cold creeping into their bones.

As dawn breaks, they crest a hill and see the faint signs of a border—rusted fencing, a sandbagged outpost. They're close to the edge of Western Sahara now. There was no sign of the train, only the prospect of a long walk ahead.

They rose before the sun.

The fire had died sometime in the night. Their clothes were stiff with sweat and sand, and the morning wind cut through the fabric like a knife. Jack didn't speak. Neither did Augustus. They packed what little they had in silence and started walking north again.

The landscape had changed.

The smooth dunes gave way to jagged ridges and dry gullies. The ground was harder now, cracked into wide plates like ancient skin. The sand was darker, greyer. Less alive.

They walked until the light turned gold behind them.

And then—at the top of a long, bare slope—they stopped.

Ahead, in the distance, stretched a line.

Not a natural one.

Rusted posts rose at uneven intervals, some bent, some leaning, all strung with sagging coils of barbed wire. Beyond it: a low cluster of stone buildings, half-buried sandbags, a flagless pole.

Jack breathed slowly. "Is that it?

Augustus nodded.

"Western Sahara?"

"Close. Maybe inside."

Jack squinted. No movement. No vehicles. But also no welcome.

"You think it's manned?"

Augustus said, "Not during heat. Maybe not at all."

They stood for a long moment, looking.

No sign of the train. It had vanished behind them, miles gone now. No tracks. No sound. No echo of its great breathing engine.

Jack said, "So we walk through?"

Augustus shrugged. "If no one stops us."

Jack exhaled, wiped the dust from his lips.

"Long way from Newcastle."

Augustus smiled. "Longer from Banjul."

They started down the slope, slow, careful steps. The desert didn't care about the line they were about to cross.

But it was there all the same.

Jack and Augustus cross into the border zone. It's eerily quiet—no patrols, no gunfire, just scattered remnants of military outposts: sandbags, collapsed fences, rusting antennae. They pass a handwritten sign in three languages warning about mines. Tension builds as they navigate carefully.

The fence meant nothing, in the end.

It was barely standing—three strands of rusted barbed wire sagging between two warped posts. Jack stepped over it without ceremony, one hand on Augustus's shoulder for balance.

There was no welcome sign. No customs booth. No checkpoint.

Only silence.

Beyond the fence, the land flattened again. A wide, sun-bleached plain littered with fragments of metal and rock. The skeleton of a radio tower leaned at a strange angle near the horizon, its cables draped like dead vines. A half-buried tire marked a faint trail through the dust.

They moved slowly.

The air felt thicker here. Not hotter, but heavier—like it carried a memory too large to hold. They passed the remnants of an old sandbag wall, long collapsed, its canvas frayed to ribbons. Beside it lay a single boot, its toe gnawed away by sun and time.

Jack muttered, "You sure this isn't military land?"

Augustus nodded. "It was. Now no one wants it."

Not long after, they reached the sign.

It was nailed to a piece of wood hammered into the ground at an angle, written in three languages—French, Arabic, and something neither of them recognised.

Jack read aloud: "Attention. Mines. Stay off the marked paths. Do not dig."

He looked around. "What path?"

Augustus was already moving forward, his steps precise. "This one."

"You see a path?"

Augustus tapped his temple. "I remember it."

Jack swallowed. "That's not the same."

Augustus didn't respond.

They moved slowly after that—no longer speaking, only breathing. Every step felt like it might matter. The wind kicked up dust devils that danced just out of reach. The sky remained impossibly blue.

After what felt like hours, the wreckage began to thin. Fewer wires. Fewer shells of machines. No bodies. Just silence and wind.

When they finally crested the next rise, the signs of life returned—small ones.

Faint smoke in the distance. A distant braying sound.

Augustus pointed. "There."

Jack followed his finger.

At the far edge of the dust, five dark shapes fluttered in the wind.

Tents.

The tents were stitched from patched tarps and weathered canvas, arranged in a half-moon around a dry stone well. A donkey stood tethered to a crooked post, chewing from an empty bucket. Nearby, an old generator chugged quietly, rattling like it might collapse any minute.

As Jack approached, a small child bolted into one of the tents. A flap moved. Then another. Within moments, five pairs of eyes emerged from the shadows.

Mostly men. All silent.

Augustus raised one hand—not waving, not aggressive. Just stillness.

One of the men, older, wearing a white turban so faded it looked grey, stepped forward. His eyes were narrow slits beneath sun-darkened brows. He said something in Hassaniya Arabic, sharp and low.

Augustus answered in the same tongue, his accent halting but functional. A back-and-forth followed—tense but quiet.

Jack stood still, waiting, watching the donkey chew on nothing.

Eventually, the old man nodded once. He turned and barked something at the others. A younger man disappeared into a tent and returned with a plastic jug and two cracked bowls. He poured water slowly. Another brought a plate of dates and flatbread.

Augustus gestured for Jack to sit.

Jack lowered himself onto a dusty mat and drank deeply. The water was warm and metallic—but clean.

"He says we can eat. We rest for one hour," Augustus said. "Then we go."

Jack tore a piece of flatbread. "He says why?"

Augustus hesitated. "He says… this place is quiet, but not safe. Too many pass through. Not all are kind."

The old man crouched beside them, watching. He spoke again, and Augustus translated.

"He says: if someone offers a ride, ask what they carry. If they do not answer, do not go."

Jack raised an eyebrow. "Smugglers?"

Augustus nodded. "Or worse."

Jack looked out at the horizon. "We're running out of ways to move."

The old man tapped his chest and said one word: "Foot, crazy man."

'Crazy Man?' Jack wondered why those words were muttered so randomly

Then he stood and walked away.

Augustus chewed slowly. "He knows the truth."

Jack glanced at the tents. "I'm not sure I want to."

The truck appeared just after dusk.

A battered white Hilux, caked in dust and patched with duct tape along the passenger-side door. The headlights flickered on and off, and the front bumper was held together with a rope. But it moved, and that was enough.

The driver said nothing as he approached. He cut the engine and stepped out—thin, sharp-featured, with cigarette burns on his shirt and hands that looked too clean for a mechanic.

Augustus spoke first, asking where he was headed.

The man answered in clipped French: "North. Dakhla. Coast."

Jack perked up. "That's it. That's where we're going."

Augustus hesitated. "We ask first."

The driver turned and began refuelling from a plastic jerrycan strapped to the back. He didn't look at them again. In the bed of the truck sat two others—both men, both silent, wrapped in scarves with only their eyes visible. One gave a single nod in their direction. The other remained perfectly still.

The old man from the tent settlement watched from a distance, arms folded, not interfering—but not approving either.

"We go," Augustus said, without looking at Jack.

"You sure?"

"No."

They climbed into the back, settling beside the crates and jerrycans. The metal floor was hot, even in the dim light. The engine wheezed back to life, and the truck rolled forward onto a narrow path of hard-packed dust.

No words were spoken.

The driver kept one hand on the wheel and the other near the gearshift. His eyes stayed on the horizon. The two other passengers stared into the dark.

The crates smelled of oil and rope. One had a stencilled code on it—no logo, no origin. The jerrycans sloshed faintly with each bump.

Jack leaned closer to Augustus. "You trust them?"

"No," Augustus said. "But they move."

They rode like that, in silence, the sky above them full of stars, the road ahead slowly vanishing into black.

The truck rolled to a halt on a stretch of hard, windblown rock near the edge of a low cliff. Below, the desert fell away into shadows and dried gullies, scattered with thornbush and debris.

The driver cut the engine and stepped out without a word.

Augustus didn't move. Jack stretched his legs, wincing. "Why are we stopping?"

Augustus didn't answer right away.

The two other passengers remained still. But then—slowly—one of them shifted his weight and leaned forward. A dark shape emerged from beneath his robe.

A rifle. Compact. Oiled. Clean.

Jack stiffened. "Augustus…"

"I see."

The man didn't point it, didn't raise it. Just laid it across his knees, his eyes hidden behind his scarf. The message was clear: he was ready, if not yet willing.

Augustus spoke under his breath. "We leave. When the truck moves."

Jack looked around. No cover. No path. The cliff edge was ten meters away, the only break in the flatness.

"Where do we go?"

"Anywhere not here."

The driver reappeared, pouring from another jerrycan. His flashlight passed across the bed of the truck. It lingered—too long—on the two of them.

He said nothing. But he saw.

Jack's heart thumped.

The wind picked up, sending a dry whisper through the low brush. One of the crates had shifted in the ride—just enough to reveal a marking underneath the dirt. A stamped emblem: faded, but recognisable.

A crescent and star. Military surplus.

Jack's voice was quiet. "This isn't just smuggling."

Augustus nodded. "I know."

The engine sputtered back to life.

The driver climbed in, but didn't shift into gear.

He was watching them in the rearview mirror.

And smiling.

The truck rolled forward again, but slower this time—idling more than driving, its tires crunching on loose gravel. The road had narrowed to a single trail, hemmed in by jagged rock and brittle scrub.

Ahead, a shallow ravine opened to the left—a drop maybe ten feet deep, with a sand-filled basin and a sloping bank that might be climbable. The only place where disappearing might make no sound at all.

Augustus tapped Jack's arm once, firmly.

Jack didn't need words.

The driver's eyes flicked back again in the mirror. That half-smile lingered.

The man with the rifle shifted slightly, cradling the weapon like a child.

Augustus said one word: "Now."

They moved at the same time.

Augustus vaulted the tailgate with a single fluid motion. Jack followed, legs clumsy, hands grabbing at the rim.

The ground hit hard.

He landed on his shoulder, rolled twice, dust clouding up around him. Augustus was already scrambling up the other side of the ravine, pulling Jack behind him.

No shouts. No shots.

Just the whine of the engine rising.

The truck didn't stop.

It sped up. Tires bit into the road, and the red glow of its tail lights faded fast, disappearing into the night without so much as a brake tap.

Jack lay flat on his back, panting, his ribs aching.

Augustus crouched above him, silhouetted against the stars.

"You good?"

Jack coughed. "Define 'good.'"

Augustus grinned and helped him to his feet.

The wind had shifted again.

There was salt in the air now.

Not much. Just enough.

The sea was near.

They walked until the sand turned to gravel.

Then, the gravel became broken asphalt. Then the smell changed—less dust, more salt. Rotting fish. Diesel. Something industrial and alive.

Jack crested the last hill with Augustus at his side and looked down on a patchwork of rooftops, crumbling concrete, and painted tin. Antennas jutted up like skeletal fingers. Palm trees bent under dry wind. In the distance, a rusted harbour clawed out into the Atlantic, its edge lined with fishing boats and trawlers blinking in the sun.

"Dakhla?" Jack asked.

Augustus nodded. "The edge of it."

The outskirts were quiet, almost rural—low buildings, plastic sheeting stretched across shacks. Children kicked a deflated ball along a cracked sidewalk. A woman balanced a sack of rice on her head and didn't look up as they passed.

Further in, the streets narrowed. French colonial facades stood beside newer brick and cement blocks, the architecture mismatched like a town built from memory and leftover parts. The signs were in three languages—Arabic, French, and Spanish—but none said "Welcome."

Every third storefront was shuttered. The rest sold phone credit, engine parts, tea, cigarettes, or prayer rugs. Music spilled from a barbershop. A soldier stood smoking outside a police kiosk, his rifle propped casually against the wall.

Augustus kept his head down.

"Lot of people here," Jack muttered.

"Too many. Not enough boats."

"Who's in charge?"

Augustus shrugged. "Today? No one. Tomorrow? Someone else."

They went by a rusted gate, behind which a group of young men sat cross-legged on plastic crates, their eyes following the street. None spoke. One bore a tear tattoo beneath his left eye.

Jack swallowed. "You sure you know where we're going?"

Augustus said, "No. But I know who to ask."

They follow vague directions to a café known for connecting people with boats to the Canary Islands. Inside, deals are made in whispers. A fixer offers them a spot on a fishing boat—but the price is steep. They have one night to decide.

The café had no sign.

Just a red curtain over the entrance and two battered plastic chairs outside, one of them broken in half. A tin lantern hung from a hook, unlit in the daylight. The smell of overcooked fish and engine oil drifted from the alley.

Augustus pushed the curtain aside and stepped in. Jack followed.

Inside: dim light, cracked walls, five tables, one fan that didn't spin. A television mounted in the corner played a silent football match. At a back table sat four men—quiet, middle-aged, with the kind of stillness that made Jack's skin crawl.

Nobody looked up when they entered.

Augustus approached the counter and said a name under his breath. "Omar."

The boy behind the bar nodded once and disappeared through a curtain.

Jack sat slowly. His hands were still shaking from the long walk, or maybe the tension of arriving. The salt in the air made his throat dry.

A few minutes later, a man emerged from the back. Thin. Grey in the beard. Blue shirt buttoned to the top. His eyes passed over Jack, then settled on Augustus.

He spoke French. "You want water or a way out?"

Augustus answered: "Both."

The man—Omar—sat down across from them, set a battered notebook on the table, and opened it. He pointed at a line. "Fishing boat. Two days. Maybe three. Small engine. Leaves before first light."

Jack leaned in. "How much?"

Omar tapped the page. "Three hundred curos. Each."

Jack coughed. "We don't have that."

Omar didn't blink. "Then you don't have a seat."

Augustus said nothing.

Omar tore a match from a book, struck it, and lit a cigarette. "Find the money by midnight. After that, you're ghosts."

He stood and walked away.

Jack leaned back, staring at the ceiling. "We're not going to find that kind of money."

Augustus's voice was calm. "I already have mine."

Jack turned. "What?"

"I saved it. From before."

Jack's stomach turned. "And me?"

Augustus looked down. "You decide."

The alley outside the café was narrow and hot, the air thick with the smell of fried fish and exhaust. Jack stood with his hands on his hips, staring at the cracked pavement. Augustus leaned against the wall, arms crossed, eyes low.

"You had the money this whole time," Jack said.

Augustus didn't look up. "I needed it. For the end."

"You didn't think I'd need to know that?"

"You didn't ask."

Jack let out a bitter laugh. "You're unbelievable."

Augustus's voice stayed level. "You have a passport. You can go to the consulate. Buy a plane ticket. Go home."

"I don't want to go home."

"Then what do you want?"

Jack opened his mouth. Closed it.

"I came all this way," he said finally. "I nearly died out there. I ran from smugglers, bled for this, lost everything back home. Don't tell me I didn't mean it."

Augustus looked at him now. "You walked the miles. But not the choice."

Jack stepped closer. "You think this is easy for me?"

"I think you never had to jump from a truck, wondering if the sand would catch you or break your neck."

The words hung in the air like smoke.

"I gave up everything," Jack said quietly.

Augustus nodded. "Then why do you still act like you have something to go back to?"

Jack turned, the anger in him boiling over with nowhere to land. He strode to the alley's end, stopped, and swung back around.

"Maybe you're right," he said. "Maybe I never really made the decision."

Augustus didn't reply.

Jack shook his head. "Enjoy your boat."

He walked away.

This time, Augustus didn't follow.

The docks were restless that night.

Wooden planks creaked underfoot, and the smell of salt, gasoline, and rotting seaweed drifted over the water like fog. Lanterns flickered in the wind. Crates were hauled, names muttered, deals whispered and then sealed with glances.

Jack stood at the edge of the harbour, hands in his pockets, staring at the silhouettes of boats bobbing in the black tide.

He hadn't said where he was going. Just left.

Somewhere behind him, a cat darted between crates. Farther down the dock, a man cursed in Spanish, arguing over fuel.

Jack sat on a crate and watched.

He didn't know how long he stayed like that. Long enough for the sky to begin turning purple. Long enough for the decision to stop being a decision and become something else.

A small boat pulled away from a lower dock. Onboard: a man, a woman, a child wrapped in a blue blanket. The engine sputtered, then caught. No one spoke. No one waved.

They disappeared into the dark.

Jack stayed there another hour.

Then he stood.

Walked back through the alleys.

Past shuttered stalls and sleeping cats and a boy curled up on a flattened cardboard box.

He reached the safehouse, a narrow concrete room near the back of the café. The door creaked when he pushed it open.

Augustus was sitting on the floor, legs crossed, coat draped over his knees. He didn't look up.

Jack reached into his pocket.

Dropped a bundle of dirhams onto the floor between them. Crumpled, dirty, just enough.

Augustus looked up, eyes unreadable.

"I sold my watch," Jack said. "And my boots."

Augustus's eyes dropped to Jack's bare feet.

"You are sure now?"

Jack nodded.

"No more pretending?"

Jack smiled, tired. "No more pretending."

The wind was colder than expected.

They met Omar in the alley behind the café just before dawn. No words were exchanged. Only a nod. A flick of the fingers. Then a slow walk through sleeping streets.

Augustus walked with steady steps.

Jack walked barefoot.

The alley narrowed into a stone passage, then opened suddenly to a cove—half-natural, half-carved by human desperation. A single boat sat low in the water, already overladen. Fifteen or more people were packed shoulder to shoulder, faces hidden beneath scarves and hoods, arms wrapped around their bundles. No one spoke.

The outboard motor hissed softly. Another man checked the fuel with a bent straw.

Omar handed their money to a boy, who counted it in the dark, then nodded. They were waved forward.

Jack hesitated only once—when his foot touched the edge of the boat, slick with salt. For just a moment, he glanced back.

No lights. No skyline. Just the low hum of a town already forgetting them.

He stepped aboard.

Augustus sat near the front, knees pulled to his chest, eyes half-closed.

The boat rocked. Someone prayed under their breath.

Jack sat.

The engine rumbled louder.

A shove.

They drifted from shore.

The land didn't wave goodbye.

It never does.

Chapter 7

Open Water

The sun rose slowly, as if it too were uncertain whether to witness what came next.

Jack squinted into the light, the pale orange sky bleeding into endless blue. The sea stretched in every direction—no landmarks, no clouds, no birds. Just water, wrinkled and indifferent, flexing gently beneath them like a vast, breathing thing.

The boat creaked with every motion. It wasn't built for this kind of journey.

Seventeen people crowded the wooden hull, pressed shoulder to shoulder. A baby whimpered. An old man coughed. The woman beside Jack clutched a plastic bag with both hands as if it held her soul.

No one spoke unless they had to.

One boy retched over the side. A boy murmured Quranic verses to himself, voice barely louder than the slap of water against the hull.

Augustus had taken off his coat and was crouched near the stern, scooping water from the bottom of the boat with a cracked plastic bowl. His movements were steady, unhurried, as if this were not the first time.

Jack kept his eyes on the horizon.

It wasn't like looking at land, where you knew where the edges were. Here, the horizon mocked you—always distant, never real. You could chase it for eternity and still arrive nowhere.

He turned to Augustus. "You alright?"

Augustus didn't look up. "I have been worse."

Jack adjusted his scarf. The salt stung his lips.

"How long do you think?" he asked.

Augustus paused. "If the sea is kind… one day."

"And if it's not?"

Augustus glanced at him then, the smallest flicker of a smile. "Then the sea will have us."

Jack didn't reply.

There was no answer to that.

The sun climbed higher. The sea brightened, but it brought no comfort.

The waves slapped harder now. A steady rhythm—not enough to panic, just enough to remind everyone that the water below was wider and deeper than thought could measure.

Most passengers had grown quiet. Even the baby slept now, nestled in a stranger's arms.

Jack sat near the bow, knees pulled to his chest, his shirt still damp with salt.

Augustus settled beside him, wordless at first. He passed over a bottle of water. Lukewarm. Shared without ceremony.

Then, softly, he spoke.

"Why did you come?"

Jack turned. "What?"

"First question," Augustus said. "Why did you come?"

Jack looked out over the water. A seagull wheeled overhead, too far to matter.

He exhaled.

"I came because I didn't know who I was anymore. Because nothing back home fit. Not my job. Not my marriage. Not even my thoughts."

Augustus nodded.

"And what did you leave?"

Jack hesitated.

"A house I never really owned. A job that made me sick. A wife who stopped looking at me like I was someone real. And my mother's ashes, still in a cardboard box."

Silence again.

Augustus watched the horizon.

"And what do you expect to find?"

Jack swallowed hard.

"I don't know."

He looked at Augustus. "Is that enough?"

Augustus smiled, faintly. "It's more than most."

They sat without speaking, the water glinting around them.

The boat creaked, and the wind shifted.

The answers hung in the air—not finished, but enough for now.

It happened just after midday.

The heat had reached that strange, windless peak where the sea felt more like a wall than a liquid—flat, gleaming, endless. The sun cooked everything it touched, and the shadows inside the boat grew sharp and small.

Then the engine coughed.

Once.

Twice.

And died.

The boat coasted forward a few more feet, then surrendered to the tide.

Silence fell, followed by murmurs. Then panic, soft and fast.

A young man stood, slipped, and caught himself. The baby woke up crying. The girl who'd been praying began to mutter louder, faster.

The captain—if he could be called that—cursed and knelt beside the motor, yanking the pull cord. Nothing. He opened the top, slapped the casing, muttered in Wolof and then French, and then Arabic. None of it helped.

Jack looked at Augustus.

He was already scooping water again.

"What's happening?" Jack asked.

"We drift," Augustus said calmly. "Until it starts."

"Until when?"

Augustus glanced at the motor. The man working on it now had a screwdriver clamped between his teeth and grease smeared across his hands. "Until."

The wind was still. The sea rolled beneath them—gentle, but no longer friendly.

A voice shouted something. Another hand struck the side of the hull.

The panic wasn't loud—it was quiet, contagious.

Water pooled at their feet, darker now.

Jack felt it touch his heel.

The engine sat open, its guts exposed to the sun, as useless as a prayer.

Chapter 8

The Irishman

They'd given up hope of moving.

The engine lay still and open, its rusting parts shining uselessly in the noon sun. The boat drifted silently, a tiny vessel lost in infinite water. Every face aboard was etched in exhaustion and fear.

Then—off the starboard bow—a small white sail appeared, flickering like a heartbeat in the glare. It grew closer, gliding effortlessly over the waves.

"What's that?" someone hissed.

Jack squinted. "Boat."

Augustus raised a hand above his eyes. "Not that one."

No engine. Only sail.

The ship glided nearer. Its deck was cluttered with nets, buckets, and an old wine-stained Irish flag. It felt absurdly calm.

On board, a man stood, chanting a mild Irish song to himself, wild hair whipping around his face like a halo. He waved one arm high, shouting—Jack could just make out the word: "Ahoy!"

Jack stood, shielding his eyes. "Irish?"

The sailboat drew up alongside their vessel. The man leaned over the rail, one hand resting on his hip, the other holding a battered mug. His beard was curly and peppered with salt; and his eyes shone with a bright, mischievous glint.

"Name's Sean, Sean O'Donnell!" he called in a thick brogue. "But everyone calls me Digger—'cause my father was a miner! What's yer story, lads?"

He made it sound like an introduction, not a rescue.

Jack blinked. "We—our engine died."

Digger laughed. It sounded like clinking glasses. He leaned closer. "No matter, boy. I got sails. I got rum. I got stories. Climb aboard!"

A few passengers gasped, then began scrambling. But then the makeshift captain began getting very animated.. Mutters turned to cheers as the engine roared into action.

Cheers from all on the boat were quickly followed by movement as the propeller began pushing water through its blades. Jack was already on the Irishman's sailboat now and before he could assess what was going on, the little boat continued on its journey, leaving Jack and Augustus in the hands of an unusually jovial Irishman.

Digger set to work immediately—shoving ropes, adjusting the sail, patting the mast like an old friend. He handed Jack a mug filled with something dark. "Black tea or whiskey, mate?"

Jack stared. "Whiskey?"

"Sure. Tea's no use out here."

Jack lifted the mug, stared at the dark liquid.

He drank. It burned in a way that felt like a promise.

Around them, the sailboat creaked into a gentle speed. The wind filled the canvas above, and they drifted slowly away.

Jack set his mug on the deck. The horizon looked different now—still vast, still lethal—but not empty.

They were no longer alone.

The wind carried them gently now.

Digger had tied off the sail and was humming an old Irish tune as he stirred something in a battered saucepan over a tiny stove bolted to the deck. The smell—fish, tomato, something vaguely heretical—drifted across the boat.

The sun was gone, dipped below the watery line of the earth, leaving only streaks of purple and orange bleeding into the black.

The sea was calm. Deceptively so.

Jack sat beside Augustus near the bow, wrapped in a coarse blanket that smelled like engine oil and cloves. Augustus's eyes were half-closed, the wind tugging gently at his curls.

Neither of them spoke.

Far ahead, low on the horizon, two blinking lights flickered in a slow, steady rhythm.

One white.

One green.

"See that?" Jack murmured.

Augustus nodded.

"Land?"

Augustus shrugged. "Maybe. Or a ship. Or a trick."

"Do you care?"

Augustus tilted his head. "Not tonight."

Behind them, Digger banged the side of the pot with a spoon. "Dinner, my boy! Mystery stew à la Digger. Eat it or I'll throw it at the next storm cloud!"

No one moved.

Not yet.

The lights blinked again. Faint. Steady. Distant.

Jack stared at them, the taste of salt thick on his lips.

He didn't believe in omens. But something inside him settled.

They were still adrift.

But they weren't drifting alone anymore.

The sea was slick with morning light, a sheet of pewter stretching in every direction. The wind had died to a whisper. The sailboat rocked gently, its canvas slack, ropes creaking with each slow rise and fall.

Digger stood near the tiller, one foot propped on the wooden rail, a battered pair of binoculars pressed to his eyes.

Jack sat on the deck, blinking the sun out of his vision. Beside him, Augustus held a cup of weak, lukewarm tea, both hands wrapped around it like it held more than heat.

"I see something," Digger said at last.

Jack stood slowly. "Land?"

Digger adjusted the focus. "Maybe. Big. Dark. Doesn't move."

He handed the binoculars to Jack, who raised them with cold, stiff fingers.

There it was.

Not an island. Not quite.

A shape loomed on the water, hunched like a crouching beast. Long and blocky, its rust-stained bulk thrust out at odd angles like broken ribs. As the boat drifted nearer, more details came into view, bent cranes, a shattered bridge, the faint ghost of white letters fading on the hull.

It was a ship. A massive freighter. Beached or wrecked. Silent.

"Holy shit," Jack muttered.

Digger grinned. "We found Atlantis, my boy. Only it's full of tetanus."

The wreck was less than a mile away now. Rust streaked its flanks like dried blood. The sun caught on shattered glass near the bridge. Birds circled it—but not many.

Digger moved to the rudder. "Let's see what's inside."

Jack glanced at Augustus.

The shape grew larger, sharper. No island. No rescue.

Just a corpse on the sea.

The wreck loomed beside them like a cathedral of rust. Digger dropped anchor just offshore, the rope groaning as it caught. The sail flapped lazily. The others stood along the rail, gazing up at the twisted iron monument with a mix of awe and dread.

They paddled over in Digger's inflatable dinghy—one oar missing, the other tied with a string. The wreck towered above them, blotting out the morning sun in jagged shadow. Close up, it was worse than they'd imagined.

Paint peeled like skin from the hull. The ship's name—Santa Lucia—was still faintly visible beneath the rot.

Digger reached out and tapped the rusted side. "She's not dead. She's just sleeping wrong."

Jack grimaced. "You have a weird relationship with metal."

The only entry was a dangling rope ladder, frayed and swinging with the tide.

Digger climbed first.

Jack hesitated, watching the boat bob behind them, suddenly small. Then he climbed.

The deck was warped and blistered, half-swallowed by sand and salt. Water pooled in the recesses. Barnacles had crept up along the railing like a disease. Jack looked around and saw old boots, a length of chain, and a bent canteen.

No signs of life.

Plenty of signs of leaving.

Inside the bridge, glass crunched underfoot. Wiring hung like vines from the ceiling. The instrument panel was stripped bare— only a cracked compass remained, spinning aimlessly.

They moved below deck with flashlights.

Storage rooms had collapsed walls, salt-eaten pipes. In one, they found crates of sealed rations—French military surplus, half-swollen from heat. Augustus shook one and nodded.

"Still food."

Jack opened a locker. Rope. A pair of heavy gloves. A flare gun with no flares.

Digger found a faded life vest, muttered, "Better than nothing," and slung it over his shirt.

They moved deeper into the freighter's belly. The smell changed—less ocean, more mould. Damp carpet clung to the floor like rotten cloth. At the end of a corridor, someone had written SORRY in what looked like red marker—or something worse.

Jack paused there. The word didn't feel like an apology. It felt like a last breath.

No bodies. But the ship wasn't empty.

Just emptied.

Jack touched the wall gently.

"People were here. Not long ago."

Digger nodded. "Weird thing about ships—they remember more than they should."

Jack didn't ask what he meant.

Some things you didn't want to know.

The captain's quarters lay high along the ship's spine, canted slightly to starboard from whatever had driven it aground. The door sagged on its hinges. Inside, the room was dim, the air thick with the sharper reek of salt and rot.

Water lapped at the floor. Ankle-deep. Cold.

The mattress had collapsed in on itself like wet cardboard. Personal items were scattered: a boot, a broken pair of reading glasses, a mug with the words Best Papa del Mar faded to a blur.

Jack stepped carefully across the warped floor.

Augustus poked through a drawer, pulling out a map smeared with mildew. He turned it once, then twice, then gave up and dropped it.

"Empty," he said.

"No," Jack said softly. "Not quite."

At the far end of the room, nailed unevenly to the bulkhead above the ruined bed, was a painting.

Oil on canvas. A rough frame made of driftwood.

It wasn't big, but it caught the eye instantly.

A man stood chest-deep in a churning sea, arms stretched upward—not in prayer, not in surrender, but in some posture between drowning and praise. His face was smudged, unreadable.

Above him, the sky was a violent mass of brushstrokes, clouds shaped like hands.

The water didn't surround him.

It consumed him.

Digger chuckled behind them. "Well, now. That's a cheerful piece."

Jack stepped closer. "What the hell is this doing here?"

"Maybe the captain was sentimental," Digger said. "Or had a sense of humour."

Augustus stared without speaking.

Jack reached out and touched the bottom edge. The paint flaked slightly. Still sticky in places.

He didn't know why he did it—but he pried it loose.

Lifted it from the wall.

Digger raised an eyebrow. "You collecting shipwreck art now?"

Jack didn't answer.

He just turned the painting over. The back was blank.

No name. No date.

The dinghy rocked gently as they paddled back toward the sailboat, the wreck growing smaller behind them—less monstrous, more hollow. The painting lay across Jack's lap, wrapped in a damp sheet torn from the freighter's stores. Its weight was oddly heavy, out of proportion with its size.

Digger climbed aboard first, securing the rope and checking the lines with a sailor's ease.

Augustus helped Jack haul the wrapped canvas over the side.

Jack didn't speak. Just stared at it.

Then, quietly, he unwrapped it.

Held it one last time.

And dropped it overboard.

The sea took it without hesitation.

Augustus watched as it sank slowly, the last visible corner of the frame catching the light before vanishing into the deep.

No one said a word.

Digger struck a match, lit the small stove, and turned on the weather-beaten radio strapped near the tiller. Static burst, then silence. He adjusted the dial carefully.

A voice crackled through—Spanish. Faint, fractured. Something about coordinates. Then: Guardia Costera…

Digger leaned closer. "They're out there. Maybe two days south."

He turned the volume down, very low.

Then looked at Jack.

"If you could pick," he said, voice even, "where would you go? Not for paperwork. Not for borders. Just go."

Jack stared at the sky. It was starting to shift again—grey clouds creeping in, the sea darkening.

"North," he said.

Augustus nodded. "North."

Digger smiled. Not a grin. Something smaller. Realer.

"North it is, lads."

He turned the sail and adjusted the line. The wind caught, soft but promising.

The boat groaned into motion.

The freighter faded behind them.

The sea opened ahead.

And the compass pointed true.

Chapter 9

The Weather Turns

The first sign was in the air.

Not in the sky—though that too had started to shift—but in the silence that filled the spaces between creaks and waves. The wind didn't vanish. It coiled. Stiffened. Grew heavy with something unnamed.

Digger stood near the bow, squinting toward the horizon. His hair whipped in the stiffening breeze, but he didn't move. Just stared.

Jack stepped up beside him. "What do you see?"

Digger tilted his head. "Nothing yet."

Augustus sat cross-legged near the tiller, watching the sail tremble. "It feels… off."

Digger finally turned. "Storm's coming."

"How bad?" Jack asked.

Digger gave no reply. He crossed the deck swiftly, hands moving fast, tightening ropes, tying down loose buckets, and lashing the gear chest shut. Without a word he reefed the sail, the canvas snapping angrily overhead.

Jack rose. "Should we change course?"

"Wouldn't help," Digger said. "Not fast enough. Not clever enough. Not in this boat."

Jack felt it now, too—the change. The colour of the water had deepened, going from blue to something almost metallic. The sky overhead turned thick with grey. The clouds weren't fast, but they were layered. Heavy. Impossibly still.

Digger adjusted a line, then looked at them both.

"Down below, there's a belt. You're going to need it. When it hits, stay low. Don't argue. Don't panic. And don't let go of anything that wants to leave."

Jack swallowed. "Do we turn back?"

Digger gave him a smile—thin, but steady. "Jack, my lad. There's nowhere to go back to."

He then paused from his prep work and began smiling. "I should have listened to my father!" he exclaimed.

"Why? What did he say?" asked Jack.

"I don't know.......I wasn't listening!" Digger said in a loud, un-mistakenly jolly Irishman way. Then laughed heartily at his own words before continuing with his preparations for what was to come.

A gust slammed the sail. The boat groaned.

The sky broke open in the distance—not with light, but with darkness.

It came all at once.

One minute, they were sailing through a rising wind, heads low, hands tight on whatever would stay. Next, the sea erupted.

The Weather Turns

Rain fell like shrapnel, horizontal and sharp. The first wave crashed over the bow, cold and fast, nearly throwing Augustus off his feet. The sail cracked like thunder, pulling hard at its moorings. Wood groaned. Rope snapped somewhere aft.

Digger fought the lines with all the speed of muscle memory. "Reef it down!" he shouted.

Jack stumbled toward him, eyes burning with salt and rain. "What do I do?!"

"Get below!" Digger shouted. "Tie down the stove—move the gear—don't stand upright!"

The boat pitched violently, a wave smashing across the port side and soaking them in one cold slap. The deck tilted at a steep angle. Augustus grabbed the tiller and held on for dear life.

Then it happened.

Another wave—taller, darker—slammed over them. Digger slipped, caught himself, slipped again. His shoulder slammed into the mast. Hard.

There was a sickening crack.

He dropped like a sack of rope.

"DIGGER!" Jack yelled, scrambling toward him.

Digger didn't answer. His eyes were closed. Blood ran from a gash above his brow.

Augustus shouted over the roar, "I can't—steer—this!"

Jack crouched beside Digger, shook him. "Can you hear me? Sean?"

Nothing.

The boat pitched again, nearly vertical. Augustus screamed something unintelligible.

Jack seized Digger beneath the arms, dragging him towards the hatch. His boots slid across the wet deck. Another wave struck, smaller, but swift and almost swept all three of them overboard.

He kicked open the hatch and hauled Digger inside, slamming it shut behind them.

The cabin tilted. Objects tumbled. A cup shattered.

Digger moaned once—then went silent.

Above, the sail flapped like a beast in chains.

Augustus was alone at the tiller, drenched and wide-eyed, mouth open in a prayer or a scream.

The sea showed no mercy.

The storm broke by morning.

It didn't end—it just unravelled. The waves became confused, scattered, and crashing from all sides. The sky stayed grey, bloated with leftover violence. The sail hung limp, torn halfway up the main seam. Salt crusted every surface. The sea was no longer a threat.

Now it was a void.

Augustus sat at the tiller, arms limp, rope burns lining his palms. He didn't look up. He hadn't spoken in hours.

Below, Digger lay curled on the floor of the cabin, breathing shallow, wrapped in a rain-soaked blanket. His left side was a bloom of dark bruises. The gash on his forehead had stopped bleeding, but only because there wasn't much left in him to lose.

Jack crouched near him, flipping through the black leather notebook Digger always kept tied to the mast.

Inside, it was worse than useless.

Smeared ink. Torn pages. Coordinates. Scribbles. Doodles of fish and boats and drunken rhymes. One page read:

"If you hit Wales, you've gone too far.

If the sea sings, drop the jar.

North by heart, West by sin.

Look for lights. Let them win."

Jack closed it.

He looked up at the sliver of sky through the hatch.

"We're adrift," he said quietly.

Augustus didn't respond.

Jack climbed out. The deck was slick and quiet. The sail flapped once, weakly.

He sat beside Augustus.

"I don't think we can steer," Jack said.

"No."

"I don't think we can fix the sail either."

"No."

They sat like that.

Two men in a boat with no engine, no sail, no direction.

Just a bruised Irishman muttering about Neptune in his sleep, and a compass needle spinning like it had a secret.

The sea rolled beneath them.

Unconcerned.

The stars came out like a bruise in the sky.

They weren't bright. The cloud cover had thinned but not cleared. Still, the constellations began to show themselves—soft pinpricks through haze, scattered across the ocean's mirrored skin.

Augustus leaned against the rail, eyes upward.

Jack sat beside Digger in the cabin, pressing a damp cloth against his forehead. Digger moaned now and then—nonsense words, Irish songs half-whispered, murmured curses at someone named "Sarah" or "the sky."

Jack looked up through the hatch. "He's not waking properly."

"He's not dead," Augustus said from outside.

"That's not the same as alive."

Augustus didn't argue.

He stood with the compass cradled in his hand, watching the arrow sway and tremble. In his other hand was a plastic water bottle, half full, warming in the air.

Jack climbed out beside him. "You doing something?"

Augustus nodded toward the sky. "Trying."

"Trying what?"

"My grandfather was a fisherman on the river. He didn't have GPS. He said if you follow the goat, the goat takes you north."

Jack blinked. "The goat?"

"Capricorn," Augustus said, as if this were obvious.

He held up the compass, compared it to the faint points of light. "That way," he said finally. "I think."

Jack looked where he pointed. It was just more ocean.

But it was better than drifting.

"Alright," Jack said. "Steer us that way."

Augustus moved to the rudder. The boat responded sluggishly, only half willing. The sail was ragged, but it still caught a breath of wind when they found the right angle.

They didn't move fast.

But they moved.

Below, Digger muttered, "Don't let the stars lie to you... The stars are bastards..."

Augustus kept his hand steady on the tiller.

Jack watched the horizon.

At least now, they had something to chase.

The Weather Turns

The sky broke open on the fifth day.

Not with light, not with storm—but with stillness. The clouds peeled back like bruised cloth. The sea flattened into a sheet of pale metal. The air felt suspended, holding its breath.

Jack woke to silence.

He stepped out of the cabin and blinked. The water was mirror-flat. The sail hung loose, torn but upright. Augustus sat at the stern, hand on the tiller, watching nothing.

"No wind," he said.

"No storm either," Jack replied.

Below deck, Digger stirred.

Jack found him propped against the side of the hull, blinking slowly, his eyes clearer than before but rimmed in yellow.

"You back?" Jack asked.

Digger smirked weakly. "Half of me. The other half's off flirting with Saint Peter."

"You can't move much."

"Nope. I'll be your ghost navigator for now. What'd I miss?"

Jack hesitated. "We followed Capricorn."

Digger coughed, then winced. "Ah. The goat trick. Not bad."

He pointed vaguely toward the bow. "Radio's dead. Flares are wet. If we're close to anyone, we'd have to shout. If not…"

He let the sentence hang.

Jack looked out at the empty sea.

"Either way," Digger said, "you're choosing who finds you. That's the only freedom you've got left."

No one moved.

Then Jack stepped out onto the deck.

He took the flare.

Looked at it

Then set it down, unused, beside the tiller.

He turned toward the sea.

"North," he said.

Augustus adjusted the rudder.

The boat eased into motion, slow, creaking, but steady.

Above them, the goat star watched.

And ahead, the sky bent gently, waiting.

They had been at sea for nineteen days.

They crossed the wide mouth of the Atlantic in silence.

The Bay of Biscay was cruel, too vast for pity. For days, they saw nothing but slate waves and bloated sky. Rain came sideways. Wind came from everywhere. Salt encrusted their clothes, their skin, even their eyelids.

Jack's knuckles cracked from the cold. His lips split when he tried to speak. His face had peeled, then hardened.

Digger had gotten sick three days in — feverish, muttering nonsense, eyes rolling like loose marbles. Jack had thought he would die sometime around the eighth day, during a storm that snapped their mainsail rope and tossed them like driftwood.

But Digger lived.

The fever broke on a morning so still it felt like a trick. He opened his eyes and croaked, "Still ugly, mate. That's a bad sign."

Jack didn't laugh.

He just handed him a flask of warm rainwater they'd caught in a broken solar panel lid.

They floated on.

Somewhere between starvation and acceptance, the sea began to speak back, not with words—but with visitors.

One dawn, when the world burned orange and the wind finally calm, a whale surfaced just meters from the hull. Its breath rose like steam from a myth. Digger, too weak to sit, watched it pass with a look of calm wonder—like a man who had seen God and remained unimpressed.

"That's the first beautiful thing I've seen since Mauritania," he said.

Another day, they were surrounded by a pod of dolphins— cutting through the surf like joy made muscle. Jack stood holding the mast, watching them circle, leap, vanish. Digger had tried to clap, failed, and coughed blood instead.

One night, phosphorescent plankton lit the water beneath them.

Jack leaned over the edge and watched his own reflection glow.

They ran out of food on the fifteenth day.

Jack chewed rope fibres to distract his hunger. Digger drank seawater once, vomited it back, then laughed like a man whose mind had finally turned to glass.

By day seventeen, they no longer expected land.

They'd stopped measuring time. Sleep became a series of blackouts. Words became gestures. The boat moved without their will, pushed by currents deeper and older than any map could name.

****

Lying on the deck, eyes directed straight upwards to the endless blue sky, Jack drifted in and out of thoughts of his past, his mind playing over scenes he had fond memories of, and also the memories he'd chose to forget.

Jack could see his father when he was still a child.

Ronnie Crane, a wise slim figure of a man. A man always doing someone a favour. A father whose eyes seemed to be always in the shadows of a worried or thinking brow.

Jack loved that man. His father, his dad. Jack wanted to grow up and be just like him. Just like Ronnie Crane. The hero in his world. Jack could see his dad Ronnie, proudly wearing his airline uniform, he loved him in that uniform.

Ronnie had been a commercial pilot—a precise, methodical man who believed the world could be managed if you just followed the checklist. He'd been flying routes for over thirty years.

Ronnie rarely spoke in emotional terms, but he showed up. That counted for a lot.

However, during a routine international layover in Dubai, following a simple gesture to a cleaner to carry her mop and bucket up a flight of stairs, Ronnie suffered three consecutive heart attacks in the airport terminal. No warning. No time to call. No final words. Just a line of bland emails from the airline, followed by a curt hospital report and a sealed casket.

Jack flew out to claim the body. Lauren offered to come—he told her not to. Something about the quiet in that hospital, the fluorescent stillness, the frozen struggling for life expression on his dad's face, just broke him in a way he wouldn't name. Jack had always seen the world as a story worth capturing. But his father's death didn't fit any frame. There was no angle. No closure. Just absence.

When he returned, he changed.

Jack turned down a full-time contract with a national paper. He stopped covering local or domestic issues. He took riskier assignments—Sudan, Syria, Myanmar, Chechnya—going places even experienced journalists avoided. His work became darker, not just in tone but in purpose. His captions grew shorter. His photos less about beauty, more about brutality. As if documenting pain was the only way to punish the world for how little warning it gave.

Lauren tried to follow. She supported him from afar at first, then in the field, flying out between assignments. But the longer Jack stayed in danger zones, the more distant he became. Not just geographically—emotionally. He stopped taking her calls when embedded. He'd vanish for weeks. When he returned, he spoke less, drank more, and always had another flight booked.

Lauren was ambitious, yes, but grounded. She believed in stories that changed things, in journalism that held power to account. Jack had stopped chasing justice. He was chasing ghosts.

The breakup wasn't explosive. She just left the flat they shared without saying goodbye. Her heart was still with him but she knew he had a journey to travel, a road to go down and she accepted he needed to go down it without her.

Now, Jack moves alone. He writes when he must, photographs when he can, lives out of a pink and black backpack once belonging to Lauren with a half-broken press badge taped to the inside. Editors still buy his stories—though often with caution. He's known for getting too close. For breaking rules. For surviving when others don't.

He hasn't spoken to Lauren in almost two years. Sometimes he sees her byline and doesn't click. Other times, he reads every word.

Somewhere in his work, he's still looking for something he lost in that hospital room. Maybe the story that'll make sense of Ronnie's death. Or maybe proof that if you stay moving, nothing can catch up with you.

A tear stung Jack's right eye.

Jack sat up, jolted by the pain. The tear causing the discomfort was far too salty.

It wasn't a tear. It was sea water. Splashes from a breaker on the starboard side snapped Jack back into reality. he sat upright, rubbed his eyes and looked across the bow, when his eyes finally adjusted,

It appeared.

A jagged green shape on the horizon.

Not a hallucination. Not a mirage.

Real.

Cliffs. Mist.

And gulls—white, circling like the breath of northern wind.

Digger was the first to spot it.

He lifted his head from the gunwale, eyes squinting, and exhaled a sound that might've been a laugh.

"Home," he wheezed. "Ugly old bastard of a place. Look at her."

Jack didn't speak.

He just gripped the mast tighter, knuckles white, body too stiff to shake.

He should've felt something.

Joy. Grief. Triumph.

But all he felt was emptiness.

Like he'd passed through too much to arrive anywhere.

They had made it.

But what had they brought with them?

Just themselves.

Just bones.

Just names that no one here would understand.

The cliffs rose out of the water like a quiet judgment.

Green and grey, wrapped in mist, studded with tufts of white gulls. Not jagged like the coasts they'd imagined, not glowing in welcome—just there. Solid. Unmoving. Real.

England.

Jack stood at the bow, eyes sunken, lips cracked. His hands clung loosely to the railing. Salt crusted every inch of his coat. He hadn't shaved in weeks. He hadn't needed to.

The wind smelled different here. Cooler. Damp. Like stone and lichen and old soil.

Behind him, Digger wheezed from his seat near the tiller. "I'd kiss it," he muttered, "but I can barely move my mouth."

Jack didn't answer.

They drifted closer, sails slack. A small motorboat approached from the harbour. Blue stripe. Official-looking. Someone waved.

Digger grinned. "If they shoot us, I die a gentleman."

The patrol boat circled, cautious but not hostile. Jack raised one hand.

Two officers called out questions in English—clipped, clear, not unkind. Jack answered slowly: name, nationality, medical needs. Digger was eased down into the boat, wrapped in a grey blanket as though he were some fragile relic.

Jack remained on the deck.

He looked back.

The sea behind them was flat, infinite.

He looked to his right.

Augustus stood silently, his arms crossed, watching the land draw near.

Jack blinked.

When he looked again, the space was empty.

Only him.

Only England.

And the tide, rolling in like an old answer.

Chapter 10

Back on Dry Land

They're taken in by a small harbour patrol off Cornwall. Authorities are curious but cautious. Digger plays the eccentric sailor role to perfection. Jack answers their questions dully. No one mentions Augustus. No one saw him.

The dock was made of concrete and quiet judgment.

A drizzle hung in the air like smoke. The harbour town stretched beyond it—slate roofs, red chimneys, the scent of fried fish and wet wool. It could've been any postcard from the edge of Britain.

But to Jack, it felt like fiction.

The harbour officers helped Digger onto a stretcher, still bundled in his blanket. He made it theatrical, groaning like a wounded pirate.

"You're gonna want to write this down," he told the nearest guard, "because it's the best shipwreck since The Odyssey."

They laughed, a little. But they didn't look amused.

Jack followed behind, hands in his coat pockets, feet bare on wet concrete. They led him to a grey building near the pier—a kind of customs hut. Warm inside, faint smell of mildew and tea.

He sat. They asked questions.

He answered.

Name: Jack Crane.

Origin: UK citizen. Passport stolen. He'd been travelling.

Where from?

He hesitated. "Mauritania."

Eyebrows lifted.

With who?

He paused again. "An Irishman. The sailor. Digger."

They wrote it down.

"Anyone else?"

Jack stared at the floor.

"No."

The silence stretched.

One officer asked, "Did you encounter any traffickers?"

Jack nodded slowly. "Yes."

"Did you board any other vessels?"

"No."

"Were there any others with you at sea?"

Jack's mouth moved before his brain. "No. Just Digger."

The pen scratched the page.

Augustus's name was never spoken.

No one asked. No one saw.

And Jack didn't offer.

Outside, a gull screeched once, sharp and brief.

The tide rolled in.

At a hospital in Plymouth, Digger—bandaged and patched—sits beside Jack as they wait to be processed. Digger casually asks: "Who is Augustus?" Jack freezes. Digger insists: "You kept talking to him, but… I never saw him. Not once."

The hospital smelled like antiseptic and overcooked soup.

Jack sat in a moulded plastic chair in the waiting area of a side wing marked Temporary Admissions – Foreign Nationals. A heater hummed in the corner. Outside, the window showed a line of hedges, wet with drizzle.

Digger sat beside him in a wheelchair, his ribs tightly bandaged, a heavy jacket draped across his lap. Someone had given him a biscuit and a paper cup of lukewarm tea, which he held like it might reveal his future.

For the first time since Mauritania, Jack felt warm.

He didn't trust it.

Digger slurped from the cup and leaned sideways, voice low. "So, My Boy…"

Jack stared straight ahead.

Digger said, "There's something I've been meaning to ask you."

Jack didn't respond.

"You gonna tell me who Augustus is?"

Jack turned.

Digger sipped again. "I mean, you kept talking to him. On the boat. In the cabin. You called out his name in your sleep. But…" He tilted his head. "I never saw him."

Jack blinked.

"You were the only one I pulled up from that smuggler's boat," Digger added. "You and your bag of sand dreams."

Silence.

Digger's tone stayed light. Curious, not accusing. "So who was he, then? Someone from before?"

Jack didn't answer.

Digger shrugged. "Sometimes the sea gives you a friend you already had in your head."

He leaned back and sipped his tea. "Not the worst thing, if he kept you sane."

Jack looked down at his hands.

He tried to remember the first time he'd seen Augustus.

The train? The checkpoint? The desert?

Or before that?

His memory bent like a spoon in heat—melting into shapes that never existed.

He closed his eyes.

Augustus's voice came to him: "We walk."

He wasn't sure if it was a memory or a mercy.

The sun was everywhere.

It poured from the sky without mercy, without shadow. The air shimmered above the sand like it was trying to flee. Wind came in bursts, lifting dust in swirls that felt like laughter.

Jack stumbled through it—barefoot, sunburned, lips split.

His backpack was dragged over one shoulder. His eyes were glassy. His breath came in ragged, wet gasps.

He hadn't seen another person in over a day.

The group he'd tried to follow—gone. A truck had broken down. Some had vanished into the dunes. He hadn't even noticed when he lost them.

The mirage began that evening, just as the light started to change.

At first, it was just a voice behind him.

"You should walk north."

Jack turned.

A figure walked beside him. A young man in worn clothes, head wrapped in cloth against the wind, sandals quiet against the shifting sand.

"You're going the wrong way," he said.

Jack squinted. "Who—?"

"The sun sets west," the man said, smiling gently. "But water lies north."

Jack nodded slowly. "You from Gambia?"

The man smiled. "Augustus."

Jack laughed, though it sounded cracked. "Alright, Augustus."

From that point on, he wasn't alone.

They shared stories—Augustus asking questions, nudging Jack forward when he collapsed. They rode the train together. Hid from guards. Found water. Slept on ore.

In memory, it was all real.

Only now, seated in a hospital in Plymouth with a bandaged Irishman and a cup of tea, did Jack realise:

There had never been another voice in the sand.

Never another pair of footsteps.

Only him.

And the part of himself that wanted to survive.

The tide was low.

Jack walked along the beach with his coat zipped high and his hands in his pockets. Pebbles clicked beneath his shoes. The sky overhead was the colour of old metal. Waves came in slowly, as if reluctant.

He passed fishermen packing up their lines. A couple walking a dog. No one looked twice at him.

England.

Cold, damp, unsentimental.

He paused at the edge of the water, let the foam lap at the toes of his shoes. Seagulls wheeled overhead, their cries cutting through the steady roar of the surf.

He closed his eyes.

He could still hear Augustus.

"We go now."

"You are sure now?"

"Then we trust north."

Jack didn't smile.

But his mouth softened.

He looked up at the sky—grey on grey. No stars now. Just clouds. But he remembered where they'd been.

He whispered, quietly: "Thank you."

A wave rolled in and tugged gently at his soles.

He stepped back.

Turned around.

And walked inland—into a country he barely remembered, toward a life that had no shape yet.

But this time, he didn't wait for direction.

He just walked.

A cold breeze blows past him and he puts both hands deep into his coat pockets.

It was only then that Jack felt it: a leather pouch. Inside the pouch were stones.

There was also a letter.

Signed at the bottom.

He held it close to his eyes to make sure what it read.

It was signed by,

Augustus.

Chapter 11

The Search For Ndangan

There was still sand in the lining of his boots.

Jack Crane sat on the edge of his narrow flat's mattress, one socked foot on the floor, one bare. The heating clicked in the walls, slow and sluggish. The January air had a clean, iron scent, like wet railings. But under it, he could still smell the desert: that dry, flat warmth that never left your lungs once you'd breathed enough of it.

The flat was quiet. Too quiet. No hum of Augustus singing under his breath. No soft words. No rasping chuckle in the dark.

Jack pulled out the old pink-and-black canvas satchel he had shoved into the wardrobe and never touched since. Inside lay a few rolled shirts, a battered notebook, and beneath them his coat; heavy, olive-drab, its fabric stiff with old sweat and salt. He spread it open slowly, the cloth hardened in places, puckered in others. When he shook it, a little cloud of dust lifted from the collar.

He sat with it across his knees for a long time.

Then, without knowing exactly why, he reached inside the left interior pocket — the one that had always sagged a bit, the seam slightly frayed.

His breath caught. He reached deeper and pinched the lining with both hands, feeling the lumpy weight shift inside it — tucked into a hidden inner pouch, one he didn't remember using. The stitching looked wrong. Not his. Tight, careful, done by hand.

129

He didn't move. Not at first. Then, slowly, he opened the drawstring.

Inside: gemstones. Rough-cut. Dull but dense with colour — greens, milky reds, yellows with veins running through like tree roots. Not polished. But real.

And beneath them, folded tightly, creased and stained:

A letter.

His throat closed.

He picked it up, heart now hammering, and turned it over.

There was a name scrawled across the back in blocky, practised handwriting. Just one word, but enough to make the bottom fall out of him:

"Jack."

The paper had the texture of something kept close to the body for too long — soft at the creases, smudged at the corners. A faint smell of smoke, or maybe sweat. Jack unfolded it slowly, flattening it on the tabletop with both hands.

The handwriting was careful, slanted to the right, as if written with painful effort. English, yes — but not native. The letters formed with that deliberate grace of someone writing their second language, trained by repetition.

He read:

"To Jack — the man dying in the sand."

I don't know if you'll live.

But I'm writing to you as if you will, because men need voices to follow, even when there's no water.

You thought I was helping you. But you helped me.

You walked with me when no one else would. You gave my story a place to go.

The stones are yours now. If you return them, do so only to the river. But if you keep them, you must carry the name of the village too.

Ndangan is not lost. Only sleeping.

But it remembers.

If the river forgets our names, then we are truly gone.

— Augustus Sanyang

The Youngest Alkalo

Ndangan Elder

(Written in my mother tongue below. For the water. Not the wind.)

Jack read it twice. Then a third time.

His hands were shaking.

Augustus. Augustus, whose cracked lips and dark laughter had walked beside him for days — whose voice had pulled him forward, through heat and blindness and the edge of madness. The friend who found the train, helped find food and water many times. The man who followed the GOAT, who navigated the waters back to England with him. The 'Angel on his shoulder'.

He had died. Jack knew that.

He had seen the skeletal remains. Slumped in the sand, flesh long since erased from the body it once covered.

And yet this… this had been placed in Jack's coat, with a pouch of stones that couldn't possibly be imagined.

Jack sat down hard, the letter spread in front of him, the table lamp throwing pale gold across the words. He reached for a drink — didn't have one. He reached for his phone — didn't want it.

He stared at the name:

Ndangan.

And whispered it once, as if afraid it might burn his tongue:

"Ndangan."

The name — Ndangan — echoed through the walls of Jack's skull like something cracked loose and rolling.

He leaned back in the chair, fingers gripping the edges of the table. The light buzzed above him. His gaze drifted, unfocused. And from somewhere deep within, the desert returned.

It didn't arrive gently.

It surged.

Heat. Heat on his back like a giant's palm. The air boiling.

He's crawling. Lips split. Skin sloughing at the shoulders.

"Drink, fool," Augustus mutters, pushing a tin cup toward his hands.

Jack remembers reaching for it, the tremor in his arm like a broken wire. He'd smelled salt — or blood — or maybe nothing.

He remembers Augustus crouching beside him, face shadowed under that wide straw hat, cheeks hollow.

"White people don't melt properly. You crack," Augustus had said, grinning.

"Bugger off," Jack rasped. "I'm elegant."

"You're boiled ham with a press badge."

They'd laughed. Hadn't they?

But now — in the memory — something flickered.

Jack saw himself. Alone. Talking to empty air. His lips moving. Laughing. Responding to silence.

A rock that had looked like a water canteen. A dead bush he thought was a man's shoulder.

Augustus. Was he there?

Or was he just constructed?

A last fire in Jack's dying mind?

Another memory:

They're sitting under the shadow of a rusted-out truck frame, half-buried in the dunes. Augustus is holding something — a small pouch. He rolls it in his palm, listens to the stones inside.

"You know what makes a stone worth more than another?" he asks, not looking at Jack.

"Colour. Density. Bribability of customs officials?"

Augustus smiles.

"No. It's the story. This one here?" he lifts a cloudy red one, "This one was born under a sleeping hippo. That's worth at least three carats."

Jack remembers laughing so hard he coughed.

But when he tries to follow the memory further, it fractures.

Was that the moment Augustus slipped the pouch into Jack's coat?

Or had Jack imagined the whole story to explain a mystery he'd never solved?

Back in his London flat, Jack lowered his head to the table.

The letter lay in front of him like an indictment. Or a prayer.

He gripped the edge of the table until his knuckles whitened, until the tremor in his hands stopped being just emotional.

Then, finally — without thinking — he whispered:

"Augustus… were you ever really there?"

From somewhere in the pipes, a groan of old metal.

From outside, a gust of wind pressed against the windows like a breath.

He closed his eyes.

And let the answer remain silent.

Lauren arrived the next morning, knocking with the soft insistence of someone who already regrets coming.

Jack opened the door shirtless, unshaven, eyes rimmed in red.

She took one look and exhaled. "You've been crying or drinking. Or both."

"I found something," he said.

"That's usually what people say before they get sectioned."

He stepped aside.

Inside, the flat smelled like a burnt kettle and three weeks of unopened windows. The table was cleared but cluttered — the leather pouch sat in the middle like some forgotten relic. Besides, it rested the letter, pinned beneath a glass ashtray Jack never used..

Lauren picked it up, casually at first — then slower, as her eyes tracked the handwriting. She read in silence. Twice. Her brow creased.

When she finally looked up, her voice had dropped a register.

"Where did you get this?"

"It was in my coat pocket."

She gestured at the gemstones. "Are those real?"

Jack shrugged. "You tell me."

She picked one up with two fingers, held it to the light. It caught a vein of sun and flickered like a damp coal.

Then she pointed at a line in the letter.

"Ndangan is not lost. Only sleeping."

"That word," she said, tapping it. "Ndangan. That's not a word someone makes up."

"I know."

She sat down. Her face had shifted — the sarcasm retreating, something quieter replacing it.

"This is West African English. I'd bet my left hand it's written by someone from The Gambia. See this phrasing — 'the river forgets our names'? That's a concept from Mandinka cosmology. Oral culture. Water is a memory-keeper."

Jack stared at her.

"So…?"

She ran a hand through her hair. "So this wasn't written by a heatstroke fantasy. Someone real wrote this. And if the gemstones are real too…"

She paused.

Jack finished the sentence for her.

"Then Augustus was real."

Lauren didn't smile. She just reached for her bag and pulled out her laptop.

"You said Ndangan?"

Jack nodded, barely breathing.

She typed in silence. Pages loaded. Tabs opened. She frowned. Then she whispered, like to herself:

"There's nothing."

Jack's heart sank.

"No records?"

"Not in English. Not in French. Not in old colonial maps. It's like the village doesn't exist. Or someone erased it."

Jack looked down at the letter.

Augustus's words came back to him.

If the river forgets our names, then we are truly gone.

Lauren tapped the table.

"Well," she said. "Let's go wake the river."

Lauren's laptop glowed like a campfire in the middle of Jack's cluttered table. The sun outside was dull and flat, cloudlight pressing against the windowpanes. The gemstones were spread out now like an offering, each one glinting dully under the overhead bulb.

"This isn't a town that was forgotten," she said. "It was scrubbed out."

Jack leaned over her shoulder, eyes tracking as she scrolled.

On the screen was a grainy scan from a 1981 academic journal — "Post-Colonial Erasures in Rural West Africa: Case Notes from The Gambia and Guinea-Bissau." In the margins, a footnote:

"Village of 'Ndangan' referenced orally by three unrelated Mandinka elders in the Kiang region. Not found on contemporary maps. Possible lost settlement pre-1974. Erased in the boundary consolidation initiative."

Lauren looked up. "Jack… That's your guy. That's Augustus."

Jack said nothing. He just exhaled slowly, like air escaping from something broken.

Lauren turned the screen toward him.

"You see this?" She pointed to a scanned map. Faded, almost skeletal, colonial French. "There was a tributary here. Runs into the Gambia River. Small inland bulge of mangrove. No name. But look." She enlarged the image — a barely legible marking in smudged graphite.

"Nda—"

The rest had been worn away.

"Coordinates?" Jack asked, his voice hushed.

She nodded. "Close enough to get us there."

He didn't blink. "We're going."

She gave a low whistle. "You really think this is more than just a dead man's story?"

Jack turned his eyes to the pouch, then the letter.

"I don't think he's dead," he said. "I think he's waiting."

Lauren stared at him for a moment. Then, finally, a smile tugged the edge of her mouth.

"I'll book the flights."

Jack blinked, like something in him unclenched.

"To Banjul?"

"No," she said. "To the place that isn't on any map."

The plane cracked open like a metal blister, and the heat rushed in like it had been waiting just behind the door.

Jack stepped out into it and staggered slightly — the sun hit him like a floodlight, wrapped in diesel exhaust, wet heat, and the salt-heavy reek of the sea. His vision blurred for a moment. Sweat bloomed instantly across his back.

Lauren was already moving ahead, sunglasses on, her ponytail dark with damp.

"Welcome back to the world," she called, her voice dry as sandpaper.

He caught up. "Feels more like stepping into someone else's fever dream."

She gave a half-smile, navigating through the small arrivals building with practised ease. "You did ask to come back to the source."

Inside, the Banjul airport was more noise than architecture — a low rumble of shouting, mechanical fans, paper signs taped over other signs. Customs lines crawled like centipedes. The power flickered once, and nobody reacted.

Lauren breezed through, flashing her press badge. Jack fumbled his way behind her, still holding the memory of Augustus's letter in his coat pocket like it might bite.

Outside, they hailed a battered green taxi with a cracked Jesus sticker on the dashboard and a horn that went off without being touched.

"Guesthouse by the docks," Lauren told the driver in rapid, practised tones. "Not the one with the pink shutters. The yellow roof."

The driver, a man with sea-grey eyes and a radio tuned to soft Mandinka guitar music, nodded without speaking.

As they drove through the city, Jack pressed his forehead against the window.

Banjul unfolded like a wound that wouldn't heal — rusty shipping containers stacked like teeth, goats trotting along median strips, children selling sachets of water through the car windows. The air was thick with fish smoke and engine fumes, and beneath it all, the faint smell of the river — ancient, murky, indifferent.

He turned to Lauren.

"You believe it now?"

She didn't look at him. "I believe there's a story."

The cab turned down a narrow street of pale concrete and wire fences. At the end: a low building with yellow tin roofing and a painted wooden sign:

"Kunda House – Rooms by the Hour or the Day."

They climbed out.

The driver waited. Lauren paid him in dalasi without counting.

The man looked at Jack before he left and said, almost too softly:

"Be careful what names you chase."

Then he was gone.

The bar was called "The Battery." A leftover from the colonial era — ceiling fans creaking, paint peeling, rum as cheap as toothpaste. It stood near the waterfront behind a half-collapsed warehouse, known mostly to stringers, fixers, and visiting journalists who'd already given up on their first assignment.

Jack leaned against the bar's metal counter, fingers tracing a ring of condensation around his beer. His shirt clung to him, damp from the walk, and his skin was starting to itch from the heat.

Lauren was a few stools down, talking to a pair of Norwegian aid workers about upriver checkpoints. Her voice was low, her posture deliberately loose. She was playing the long game — casual curiosity, not interrogation.

Jack was not built for the long game.

He turned to the bartender, a wiry man in his fifties with an emerald tooth and a quiet manner.

"You ever heard of a village called Ndangan?" Jack asked.

The bartender kept drying the same glass. His movements didn't stop, but something in his eyes did.

"Where?"

"Ndangan. Supposed to be upriver. Maybe south of Kiang."

A beat.

The bartender set the glass down.

"No such placc," he said.

"Sure?"

"No such place," he repeated, louder. Then walked to the other end of the bar.

Jack blinked. Turned to check the room.

A man sitting alone at the far table — a local in a grey shirt, reading a newspaper — folded it abruptly and stood. He didn't look at Jack. Just walked out the door, silent.

Lauren reappeared at Jack's side a moment later, her smile gone.

"What did you say?"

"I asked about Ndangan."

Her eyes narrowed.

"Jesus, Jack."

"What? Isn't that what we're here for?"

Lauren leaned in, her voice barely above a whisper. "You don't say names like that out loud. Not before you know what they mean. It's not just superstition. Names are dangerous here. They carry memory."

Jack looked toward the empty doorway where the man had left.

"They act like I asked about a ghost."

Lauren finished her beer and dropped a few dalasi coins on the counter. "Maybe you did."

The National Archives were housed in a squat concrete building that looked like it had been abandoned mid-construction and later reoccupied by termites. Above the front desk, a ceiling fan turned so sluggishly it might have been drunk.

Jack and Lauren were the only visitors.

The archivist, an older woman in a purple blouse and bright green scarf, eyed them with mild suspicion over her reading glasses.

"Ndangan?" she repeated, typing it into an ancient desktop computer. The keys clicked like bones. "What sort of name is that?"

"Might be Mandinka," Lauren said. "We're not sure. It's a riverside village. Or was."

The woman pursed her lips. "I've worked here for thirty years. Never seen it."

Jack tapped his finger on the counter. "Any records from the Kiang district before 1975?"

She frowned. "Some. Mostly in French or Wolof. The British files are worse — poorly scanned or misplaced. You looking for a person or a place?"

"A man," Jack said, "who might've come from there. Augustus Sanyang."

The name hung in the air.

Nothing moved.

The woman looked up, slowly. Something shifted behind her eyes. Not recognition — not exactly — but wariness.

"Sanyang's a common name," she said. "Too common to be useful."

"But if there was a record of a village with that name…"

"There isn't." She shut the drawer with more force than necessary. "You won't find it here."

Lauren stepped forward, calm but firm. "Do you know anyone who might have more… oral knowledge? A cultural historian, or—?"

The woman hesitated. Then, she reached under the desk and pulled out a handwritten list of university contacts. She circled one with a blue pen.

"Dr. Fatou Njie. Teaches at the university. Linguistics. Oral preservation. She collects things… others forget."

She slid the paper across the desk.

But as Lauren reached for it, the woman placed a hand over hers.

"Don't ask her to remember too loudly."

Lauren blinked. "Why?"

"Because some names are left behind for a reason."

The University of The Gambia campus was quiet under a gauzy late-afternoon haze. Students lounged beneath neem trees, laughing in soft bursts of English, Wolof, and Mandinka. Laundry flapped from dormitory windows. The buildings were modest — flat-roofed, sun-bleached — but the air carried a sense of intellectual friction, like too many questions crowded in a place too small to contain them.

Fatou Njie's office was on the second floor of the Linguistics wing — small, no air conditioning, filled with more books than furniture. The scent of old paper clung to the room like incense.

She didn't look like Jack expected.

She wore jeans, a navy tunic, wire-rimmed glasses, and a steady gaze that could've belonged to either a nun or a prosecutor. When Lauren introduced them, Fatou simply nodded and gestured for them to sit.

Jack unfolded the letter carefully and placed it on her desk, alongside the leather pouch.

Fatou read in silence.

Her eyes didn't widen, but they sharpened — pupils narrowing with recognition, not surprise. When she reached the end, she turned the page over, examined the back, and then returned to the beginning.

She read it again.

Finally, she spoke.

"This handwriting was learned in a British school. But the phrasing — it's… old. Like someone taught to write in English, then thought in Mandinka."

Jack leaned forward. "So he's real."

Fatou gave him a look. "Someone wrote this. And they were Mandinka. That much I'll say."

She picked up the gemstone pouch and tipped it into her palm. One by one, she let the stones spill across her desk — examining them like she'd handled hundreds before. She stopped on a pale green one, milky and chipped.

"This one's from the riverbeds. We call them sleeping stones. They come up during droughts."

Jack swallowed. "Does the name 'Ndangan' mean anything to you?"

Fatou didn't answer right away.

Instead, she leaned back, interlacing her fingers.

"I've heard it once. Only once. From a woman who was interviewing tribal elders in Kiang. It was in a list of places they said used to be."

Jack and Lauren exchanged a glance.

"Used to be?" Lauren asked.

Fatou nodded. "It was struck from government records during the late seventies. The official reason was 'redundancy' — too small to justify resources. But unofficially…"

She hesitated.

"What?"

"They say the river swallowed it. Not with a flood. With time. The people disappeared. Or were made to disappear."

Jack's stomach clenched. "Why?"

Fatou picked up the letter again and tapped a line near the bottom.

Ndangan is not lost. Only sleeping.

She set it down gently.

"Because no one likes remembering the places that refused to disappear properly."

Then, softer:

"I don't recommend you keep looking."

Jack straightened. "Why?"

Fatou stood and walked to the window. The sun was low now, bleeding orange over the rooftops.

"Because remembering can be mistaken for provocation," she said. "And provocation gets people disappeared. Even now."

The sun was beginning to sag into the trees as Jack and Lauren stepped out of Fatou Njie's office. The air had cooled a little, but it carried a thick stillness — like the city was holding its breath for the night to come.

They walked in silence through the courtyard.

Jack's jaw was tight. Lauren could feel it in the rhythm of his steps — each one like he was trying to grind the past into dust beneath his boots.

"She knows more," he finally muttered. "Fatou. She knows more than she's saying."

"Of course she does," Lauren said. "But she's survived this long by knowing what not to say out loud."

They were halfway to the campus gate when a soft voice stopped them.

"Excuse me," it said.

They turned.

A woman stood by the edge of the walkway, half in shadow. She wore a dark blue cleaning apron and carried a mop that looked too clean to be real. Her face was older than it seemed — smooth, but with the kind of stillness that comes from years of not being noticed.

She spoke to Lauren, her eyes flicking toward Jack but not resting on him.

"You are looking for the forgotten village."

Lauren paused. "Yes."

The woman nodded once, like she'd already known.

Then she glanced behind her — toward the building they'd just left — and stepped closer.

She said something in Mandinka, voice hushed.

Lauren's brow furrowed. She answered slowly, uncertain. Another exchange — brief, quick, almost invisible. Jack couldn't catch more than a word or two.

Then the woman looked him dead in the eyes and said in English:

"My grandmother was born in Ndangan. She used to sing the river's name in her sleep."

Jack's chest tightened. "You know where it is?"

The woman didn't answer.

Instead, she pulled a torn scrap of paper from her apron pocket. Folded. Weathered.

She handed it to Lauren.

A single name written in ink:

Jatto

"That's all I can give," she whispered. "He knows the river's paths. The ones that remember."

Jack stepped forward. "Where do we find him?"

But the woman was already moving — mop in hand, vanishing into the corridor like a whisper in reverse.

Lauren stared at the paper.

"Jatto," she said aloud. The name felt solid. Heavy.

Jack looked past her, toward the darkening trees, in the direction of the river.

"Then that's where we go next."

The ferry market at the edge of Banjul wasn't really a market. It was a mess.

A collection of blue plastic tarps, sun-faded umbrellas, buckets of drying fish, and rusted metal laid out in semi-intentional rows like offerings to a god of salt and chaos. The scent of brine, old oil, and overripe fruit tangled in the humid air. Radios blared mbalax rhythms beside vendors shouting in Wolof and Mandinka.

Lauren walked ahead, scanning for a familiar face. Jack followed, shielding his eyes from the low sun. He carried the folded letter in his jacket pocket as if it were made of glass.

They passed a meat stall where goats were skinned in real time beside knockoff trainers and bootleg DVDs. Lauren didn't slow. She moved like someone who knew how not to be noticed.

A few children ran beside them, hawking lighters, flash drives, and bags of boiled peanuts. Jack waved them away, his mind elsewhere.

They spotted the old fixer beneath a canvas tarp, chewing on a stalk of sugarcane and eyeing the traffic with the weary suspicion of a man who had already refused everything.

"Baba!" Lauren said, crouching beside him. "Still keeping your eyes on the river?"

The man squinted, then gave a slow, toothy grin. "You again. I thought they deported you."

Lauren smirked. "Not yet. I'm still charming."

Jack hovered beside her. Baba gave him a once-over.

"You bring a ghost with you this time?"

Lauren lowered her voice. "We're looking for a man named Jatto. Might run a boat. Might live near Lamin Lodge."

The man's eyes narrowed.

"You don't want Jatto."

"I really think we do."

Baba sucked on his cane for a moment, then spat.

"Jatto doesn't take jobs. He takes on debts. You don't pay with money. You pay with time, or blood, or a piece of yourself you forgot you needed."

Lauren stayed quiet.

Finally, Baba shrugged.

"He fishes by the mangroves. Past Lamin Lodge. Down where the water bends like a hook. The boat looks like it should've sunk years ago. So does he."

Jack leaned in. "Why would he know about Ndangan?"

Baba didn't flinch — but he did stop smiling.

"You're chasing the village with no shadow," he said.

Jack nodded.

The fixer leaned back, sighed through his nose.

"If you find it," he said, "don't look directly at it. And don't take anything back that breathes."

Then he turned back to his sugarcane.

The road to Lamin Lodge gave up halfway through being a road.

Jack and Lauren walked the last mile on foot — sand, broken concrete, goat droppings, and mangrove roots clawing across the path like fingers trying to reclaim it. The sun was low but heavy, soaking their clothes, drawing salt from their skin.

The trees thickened until the river came into view — broad and dark, oil-smooth beneath the canopy. Herons stalked the shallows, necks like question marks.

Then they saw the boat.

It barely qualified. Rust-bellied, green paint peeled to the bone, half-covered in mosquito netting and tin sheets. It listed slightly, tethered to a knotted branch like a dog resigned to its chain.

Beside it, knee-deep in the water, stood Jatto.

He was taller than Jack expected, but gaunt — built from knotted tendon and ropey muscle, every inch of him the colour of smoked teak. A long beard curled along his jaw, salt-and-pepper in the sun. One leg braced awkwardly against the boat's hull, wrapped in leather and cloth. A bone pendant hung around his neck, carved into the shape of a fishhook.

He didn't look up as they approached.

Lauren cleared her throat.

"Jatto?"

Still no glance. Just a grunt and the sound of dripping net as he hauled it in, knot by knot.

She tried again. "We were told you might help us reach—"

"I don't help people," Jatto said, without turning.

Jack stepped forward. "We're looking for a village."

Jatto turned then — slowly, deliberately.

His eyes were yellowed at the edges, sharp and dry. He looked Jack up and down, then Lauren. His lip curled faintly.

"You two look like a pair of sandals that wandered off from their owners."

Lauren said, "We can pay."

"I didn't say anything about money." He limped a step forward, resting his weight on the boat. "You're not looking for a village. You're looking for a ghost. Say the name."

Jack hesitated. Then said it.

"Ndangan."

Jatto clicked his tongue, shook his head, and laughed — not kindly, more like someone hearing an old lie recited by a child.

"That place doesn't exist," he said. "And if it does, it wants to stay gone."

Lauren stepped closer. "But you know where it used to be."

"I know where a lot of things used to be. That's what old men are for. Doesn't mean I point white people toward them every time they show up with sunburn and questions."

Jack's jaw clenched. "This isn't curiosity. A man named Augustus Sanyang died trying to get out of that village. He left this behind."

He reached into his coat and pulled out the folded letter.

Jatto's eyes followed the movement. His mouth stopped curling.

He didn't take the letter. Not yet.

But he didn't turn away either.

Jack held out the letter, careful not to let his hands tremble.

Jatto stared at it a long time before finally reaching out — two fingers, callused and deliberate. He lifted the paper as though it might bleed at his touch.

He didn't unfold it immediately. He turned it over, saw the name written across the back.

"Augustus Sanyang," he murmured.

His voice didn't carry surprise. It carried memory.

He opened the letter and read. His lips moved, barely. His eyes tracked slow, steady lines. Every so often, they paused on a word like it had scraped something raw inside him.

When he finished, he stood still for a while. No wind. No breath. The river behind him moved like a thought beneath the surface.

He folded the letter once, twice, and handed it back without a word.

Lauren studied his face. Something had gone distant in it. Not absent — just turned inward, like a man watching his own past from the outside.

"Who was he to you?" Jack asked.

Jatto rubbed a hand across his beard.

"He was brave. Or stupid. Same thing when you try to walk two worlds."

"And Ndangan?"

Jatto didn't answer immediately. He limped to the boat, leaned against its side, and scratched at a rust spot with his thumb.

"My younger brother," he said finally, "was named Musa. He heard about the village from a teacher who once tried to map the river tribes. Musa was obsessed. Thought it was some Eden buried in politics. A secret exile that could be brought back."

Jatto looked at the trees, not at them.

"He went looking for it twelve years ago. Took a small boat. Said he'd be back in a week."

Jack waited.

Jatto's eyes hardened.

"He never came back."

Silence bloomed wide. Even the birds had gone still.

"Did you look for him?" Lauren asked gently.

Jatto smiled bitterly. "I looked. The river gave me back a piece of his paddle and nothing else."

He turned to Jack.

"So now you show me this letter. Same river. Same stones. Same madness."

Jack stepped forward. "Then help us finish what they started."

Jatto stared at him for a long time.

Then he said, flatly:

"I'll take you as far as the river lets me. But after that—" he pointed at the treeline, toward something only he could see, "—the path belongs to the forgotten."

Banjul's night markets hummed under lanterns and cigarette glow.

Lauren bartered for dried cassava, water sachets, and a rolled mosquito net that stank of vinegar. Jack packed quietly — flashlight batteries, a machete for weeds, a worn medical kit he hadn't used since Syria.

No phones. No GPS. Jatto had been clear: the river didn't like satellites watching it.

Their bags were light by design. One waterproof duffel each. Jack stuffed the gemstones into a side pocket without thinking, then hesitated. He drew them out again, wrapped them in cloth, setting them near the top. They weren't his, not really.

By the time they reached the mangroves again, the stars had come out.

Not city stars — real ones. Wild and ancient and countless. A full sky, laid out like a map no one had ever bothered to follow.

Jatto stood by the boat, already barefoot, already silent.

He lit the lantern without speaking.

The flame caught slowly, uncertain. It seemed to hesitate before offering light.

Lauren stepped aboard first. The boat shifted slightly under her weight.

Jack followed. The river lapped at the hull — not like a sea or a stream, but like a slow tongue remembering.

Jatto stepped in last, the boat creaking around his bad leg. He took the pole and pushed off.

No engine. No paddles.

Just the pole. Just the current.

The mangroves swallowed them quickly. Black branches above. Murky reflections below. The world collapsed into water and wood.

Jack looked back once, but the shoreline was already gone.

Jatto spoke, voice low and even:

"From here on, we follow what remembers us."

Chapter 12

The River

The river turned silver before the sky did.

Jack sat in the boat's bow, shoulders stiff, eyes fixed on the water's endless coil. The current had slowed, thickened, and become syrupy in the early morning stillness. Fog drifted low over the surface, clinging to the mangroves like gauze.

Jatto had stopped humming.

That was the first sign.

The second was the sudden smell of smoke — not wood smoke, but something acrid, electric. Diesel.

Then the sound. A low clank. Metal against metal.

Lauren leaned forward. "What's that?"

Jatto didn't answer.

Around the bend, a shape emerged — first shadow, then structure.

A checkpoint stood partly on the riverbank, partly on barrels and planks lashed together. A ramshackle post, afloat yet armed, its timbers bleached by sun and rain, draped with coiled rope and frayed strips of netting. Overhead, a Gambian flag fluttered from a rusted pole.

Two men stepped out of a shack as they approached. Uniforms not matching. Rifles did.

They raised their hands. Not waving.

Stopping.

Jack felt the tension move through Jatto's spine like a wire tightening.

The boat slid closer.

One of the men shouted in Wolof.

Jatto raised a hand and replied — calm, flat, unbothered.

The boat bumped gently against the dock.

The taller soldier motioned them to step off.

Jack glanced at Lauren. She was already slipping her camera into her pack, tucking the flap down. Eyes alert, posture neutral.

Jatto turned back to them and said, quietly.

"Let me talk. You don't know which lies they already believe."

Then he stepped onto the dock.

Jack followed.

The wood flexed under his boots. He smelled fish, gun oil, and something else—mildew or sweat. A generator choked somewhere behind the shack.

The second soldier stepped forward. Younger. Cleaner uniform. His eyes didn't blink much.

"You're not from here," he said to Jack. It wasn't a question.

Jack nodded. "No."

"What are you doing this far out?"

Jatto answered before Jack could.

"We're traders. Pilgrims, of a sort."

"Pilgrims?" the man repeated, eyebrow cocked.

Jatto grinned, as if telling a joke only the river understood. "The kind that collect stories instead of sins."

The man didn't smile.

The other soldier lifted his radio but didn't speak into it.

Jack felt the heat gathering behind his ribs.

This wasn't curiosity. This was the kind of silence that comes just before decisions are made.

And not all of them are kind.

The younger soldier stepped closer, boots loud on the makeshift dock. His rifle wasn't pointed, but it wasn't resting either.

"Passports," he said.

Jatto reached into his satchel and handed over a worn card with a red thumbprint and faded lettering.

Lauren produced her UK passport, her press credentials tucked neatly inside. She handed it over without comment.

Jack hesitated — then followed.

The soldier examined each document with exaggerated slowness, pretending to read more than he did. His eyes flicked up at Jack.

"Why are you here?"

"Documenting oral traditions," Lauren answered smoothly. "Language preservation. We're academics. Sort of."

"Tourists with notebooks," Jack added, attempting humour.

The soldier didn't laugh.

His eyes narrowed. "This far upriver?"

Jack shrugged. "We're chasing a name."

That word — name — snagged in the air like a thorn.

The soldier tilted his head.

"What name?"

Jack's mouth opened before he could stop himself.

"Augustus."

Jatto's shoulders went visibly stiff. Not dramatically — just enough that Jack saw it.

The soldier's expression didn't change, but something in his stance did.

"Augustus, what?"

Jack faltered.

"Augustus Sanyang," Lauren said, stepping in quickly. "A subject. From a local myth we're tracing. Possibly fictional. Possibly misremembered."

The soldier looked at her. "Why would a white woman come here to study a myth?"

Lauren's voice didn't flinch. "Because our country doesn't have many left."

He stared at her longer than necessary.

Then looked down at her press badge.

"What agency?"

"Independent," she said. "Freelance. You can call the British consulate if you want to waste your afternoon."

Behind them, the other soldier muttered something in Mandinka. Jatto replied in a clipped tone Jack didn't catch — but whatever it was, it made the younger one pause.

He studied them for another few seconds.

Then said, flatly: "Empty your bags."

Jack dropped his satchel onto the table with a thud.

The soldier unzipped it himself.

First came a water filter. Then a notebook. Then a pouch of dried cassava.

Then — the gemstones.

Jack hadn't packed them deeply enough. One had come loose from its wrapping and rolled slowly across the table, like an eye that refused to look away.

The soldier grabbed it.

"What is this?"

"Stone," Jack said. "Semi-precious."

"Illegal?"

"No."

The soldier turned it in his hand, as if trying to conjure meaning from its texture.

Then he looked at Jack — not suspicious now, but interested. Almost hungry.

"You found these upriver?"

"No."

"Then why are you bringing them there?"

Jack hesitated.

Lauren jumped in. "They were passed down from a source. Part of the oral history we're following. We're not here to sell them."

The soldier held the stone between two fingers. "These don't belong to you."

"They don't belong to anyone," Jack said.

Jatto stepped forward then — slow, deliberate, but his body language had changed. His hand rested near his belt, not on a weapon, but close enough to suggest intent.

"You don't want to keep that," he said.

The soldier turned. "Why?"

Jatto looked at him with dry, amused contempt. "Because that one was pulled from under a sleeping hippo. And that one—" he pointed to another, still wrapped — "was cursed by a woman whose husband never came back from a village that doesn't exist. Stones remember. Hands forget. And sometimes they take fingers with them."

The River

A pause.

Then a voice from the shack cut the tension.

"Leave it."

The soldier turned, frowning.

A second man emerged — older, taller, darker-skinned, wearing a short-sleeved officer's uniform with clean boots and a machete strapped to his back.

He walked slowly, assessing the scene.

The younger soldier stepped back, placing the gemstone down a little too quickly.

The officer looked at Lauren. Then at Jack. Then at Jatto.

"Let them pass," he said.

"But sir—"

The officer raised a hand. "I know the name they're chasing."

Jack's heart stumbled in his chest.

The officer looked at him directly.

"If the river gave you that name, it already knows you're coming. We don't need to follow."

He stepped aside.

Jatto gave the soldier a smile that showed no teeth. "You can keep the hippo stone," he said. "It'll keep you company when you sleep."

They pushed off moments later.

No one spoke.

Not until the checkpoint disappeared behind fog and vines.

The boat drifted back from the dock in a hush of water and wood.

Jack turned once more.

The senior officer stood alone now, at the edge of the makeshift checkpoint, arms crossed, machete glinting at his side.

The fog curled around him, river-thick and slow, like it didn't want to let him go.

As their boat slipped farther from the dock, he called out — not shouting, just loud enough to pierce the fog:

"You follow voices into the bush, don't expect an echo."

Jack froze.

The officer stepped closer to the edge of the dock. His face was unreadable. His voice, measured.

"The men who find that village don't always come back with their names."

Lauren turned in her seat. "You've heard of Ndangan."

He didn't nod. He didn't deny it either.

"You are beyond our protection now," he said. "What you find beyond this bend is none of our business. It stopped being anyone's business a long time ago."

Jatto didn't look back. He pushed the boat forward with the pole, using short, precise strokes.

The current took them gently, almost kindly.

The officer raised his hand — not as a wave, but a farewell.

Not see you later.

Goodbye.

Then the checkpoint disappeared behind the mist.

They drifted for what felt like hours.

The checkpoint was gone. Erased. No sound behind them, no wake, no proof it had ever been there at all.

The river narrowed until the mangroves leaned overhead, knotted together like fingers clutching a secret. The sunlight thinned into ribbons. The air cooled, but the humidity thickened, coating their skin like a film.

Even the insects were quiet.

Jatto no longer used the pole — the river was moving of its own will now, gently steering them through the maze like it had made up its mind.

Jack sat at the prow, knees drawn to his chest. The gemstones were stowed in his pack, yet he still felt their weight. He kept picturing the soldier's face at the mention of Augustus; not confusion, not surprise.

Recognising something he'd been told not to believe.

Lauren pulled out her notebook but didn't write. She just watched the trees — the way they grew in on themselves, as if recoiling.

"Jack," she said softly.

He looked over.

She hesitated. Then: "What if we find nothing?"

He opened his mouth.

Closed it.

"I don't think we're here to find something," he said.

"Then what?"

He turned back to the water. It was almost black now, reflecting nothing.

"We're here so it can find us."

Jatto muttered something behind them. Neither of them caught the words.

The trees closed tighter. The light vanished altogether.

They kept drifting — silent, slow, swallowed.

And then the river bent again, toward somewhere no compass could reach.

The river no longer flowed — it strained.

The boat pushed through thick water that clung like syrup. Roots webbed across the surface, gripping the hull like fingers trying to hold it still. Leaves hung in clusters, slick with dew and insect spit. The sun barely touched the surface now. It filtered through the canopy in shards — thin, greenish, like light passing through wine bottles.

Jack ducked a low branch. It brushed his shoulder, scattering tiny ants across his collar. He didn't flinch.

Jatto moved like a man who wasn't steering a boat but navigating a memory — quiet, leaning forward, eyes narrowing at invisible signs. Every few minutes, he reached into a pouch and pulled out something wrapped in cloth and string: a small bundle, sometimes with bone or dried leaves tied to the end. Without a word, he hung it on a branch beside the path.

Lauren finally asked, "What are those?"

Jatto didn't look back. "Markers."

"For us?"

"No. For the river. So it knows I'm not stealing anything."

Jack stared at one as they drifted past — a cluster of twigs tied with red thread, something soft stuffed inside.

"They look like charms."

"They are," Jatto said.

"What's inside them?"

"Names."

Jack met Lauren's eyes. She didn't ask more.

The boat scraped the edge of a submerged log. A chorus of frogs jumped away in unison.

They moved on.

The water narrowed further. The channel was no longer wide enough for two boats, even if they'd met one. But they wouldn't.

No one else came this way.

It wasn't on any map.

It didn't want to be.

The water changed before they noticed it had.

It wasn't just slower — it was aware. That's how Jack would describe it later, though it didn't make sense. The river seemed to be listening. Each ripple was a breath, each current a glance.

The first thing they passed was a bundle of feathers lashed to a floating stick, bobbing gently in the current. It spun slowly as they passed, without wind.

The second was worse — a doll, straw and fabric, soaked in mud and bloated with moss. Its stitched eyes stared straight up at the canopy.

Lauren reached for her camera, then stopped. Her hands were suddenly shaking.

Jack saw it too. "Why would that be here?"

Jatto didn't answer. He was steering slower now. The pole dipped in and out of the water like a tongue testing for poison.

Then came the third.

A small sandal, no longer than Jack's palm. Wedged between the roots of a tree, caught on a knot of reeds. Faded pink. A cartoon rabbit barely visible on the insole.

Lauren broke the silence. "That's a child's."

Jatto said nothing.

Jack turned in his seat, eyes scanning the branches.

He didn't see anything.

But he felt something.

Pressure. Watching. Like they were being observed not from a single point, but from everywhere at once. From the branches. From beneath the boat. From behind their backs and just beyond their ears.

He opened his mouth to say so — but nothing came out.

Not fear.

Not certainty.

Just a kind of quiet confirmation, as if the river had leaned in and whispered:

Now I see you.

The heat pressed down like a second river.

Jack's eyelids sagged as the boat rocked gently beneath him, the creak of wet wood and the rhythmic dip of Jatto's pole hypnotic. His neck tilted forward, chin brushing his chest. The sounds around him faded — the frogs, the insects, the sighing of reeds against the hull — all melted into a single slow hum.

His vision dipped, went soft at the edges, then—

He was standing.

Not in the boat. In the water.

Calf-deep. The river glassy and silent.

Everything was green — the sky, the trees, the light. A filtered world, underwater though he breathed like air.

Then he saw him.

Augustus.

Standing just a few meters away, half-submerged, arms at his sides.

He looked alive. Not clean or restored — still gaunt, skin drawn tight — but aware. Whole. Watching.

"Jack," he said, voice low, crackling like sun through leaves.

Jack couldn't speak.

"You're almost there," Augustus whispered.

His eyes — dark, full, unblinking — seemed to hold something older than memory.

He took one step forward, the river not rippling around him.

Jack tried to move, to reach, but the water clung too tightly.

Then Augustus smiled — just barely — and said:

"Don't ask the river questions you don't want the answers to."

Jack opened his mouth—

And snapped awake.

His head jerked up. His heart hammered.

He was in the boat again. The sky had dimmed — not night, but late, the light sickly with dusk.

Lauren looked over. "You okay?"

Jack wiped his face. His palm came away cold.

"Yeah," he lied. "Just dreaming."

Jatto didn't speak.

But his eyes met Jack's in the reflection off the water.

And for just a second, it felt like he knew.

The boat jolted to a stop, jerking sideways with a sharp groan.

Jack grabbed the edge to steady himself. Lauren braced against the seat. Something below had taken hold — not a log, not silt.

Jatto hissed through his teeth.

"Stay still," he muttered.

He slipped the pole into the boat, tied it off, and without another word, swung one leg over the side and slid into the river.

The water swallowed him slowly, up to his waist, then his chest.

He moved carefully, hands feeling along the hull.

Then his fingers dipped below the surface — and froze.

For a moment, he didn't move. Then he inhaled slowly and plunged his arms down, tugging, careful but deliberate.

Jack leaned over the edge.

Through the water, murky and dark, he saw something rise — tangled in weed and net, sloshing upward with a sickening drag.

Bone.

A long forearm. Discoloured ivory threaded with root and twine. The fingers still curled. One was missing at the second knuckle.

Jatto brought it out gently, holding it close to his chest as if it might fall apart.

A second bone surfaced — a partial rib — lashed to the net like it had grown there.

And around what must have once been a neck: a necklace.

172

Jack recognised it instantly.

Rough-cut stones, dull red, threaded on old cord.

The same kind as in the pouch Augustus left him.

Jatto stared at it.

The expression on his face didn't change — not grief, not fear.

Just a terrible, motionless recognition.

Lauren said softly, "Jatto…"

But he didn't answer.

He untangled the net with careful fingers, pulling loose what remained of the human shape — not enough for a body, but too much for a ghost.

Then he whispered something in Mandinka and cradled the bones against his chest.

He climbed back into the boat without looking at them.

Jack and Lauren moved aside, silent.

Jatto set the bones on a cloth and wrapped them with reverent precision.

Then he sat down, wet clothes clinging, and stared into the dark.

He still said nothing.

But Jack could feel the truth radiating from him like smoke:

He had found his brother.

The boat scraped gently against the muddy shore.

Jatto didn't speak. He gathered the wrapped bones in his arms and stepped out into the shallows. The sky was bruising overhead — not yet night, but close. The kind of dusk that made shapes blur and shadows breathe.

Jack and Lauren remained in the boat.

Jatto climbed a small rise above the waterline, where dry branches littered the slope and an old termite mound leaned like a broken monument.

He knelt.

With practised hands, he stacked kindling and dry reeds. He placed the bundle in the centre, unwrapped but undisturbed. The bones were laid like memory — careful, imperfect, intimate.

No prayer.

No words.

He struck a match from his satchel and held it until it burned his fingers.

Then he dropped it into the pyre.

The fire took quickly, coughing smoke into the trees.

Jack watched from below. The smell hit hard — not just wood, but the sour bite of age and something older. A death not grieved until now.

The flames danced quietly.

Jatto stood motionless, outlined in orange and shadow. His face was unreadable. Not stony — just beyond reach.

Lauren put a hand on Jack's arm, but said nothing.

The fire burned for an hour.

No animals called. No wind stirred the trees.

When the last ember faded, Jatto took a charred stick, stirred the ash, and scattered it into the river with a flat sweep of his arm.

Then he returned to the boat.

He climbed in, dripping and coated in smoke, and took up the pole again.

Still not looking at either of them, he said:

"Now we go the rest of the way without names."

Then he pushed them back into the dark.

The map said two forks.

Jatto had warned them: one bend sank into marshland, silt-choked and humming with mosquitoes. The other traced the old fishing line, where the river thinned and bled into a hidden place — the way to what had once been Ndangan.

But now there were three.

The tributary had split like a cracked tooth — three mouths yawning open where there should've been two. Each one nearly identical: tight mangrove arches, shallow water, dark beyond sight.

Jatto pulled the boat into a slow spin, eyeing each mouth like he was reading a warning written in bark.

"This wasn't here," he muttered.

Jack leaned forward. "What do you mean?"

175

Jatto pointed with the pole. "There are only two splits. Always been. One safe. One not. But this?" He looked around. "This is the river testing me."

Lauren opened her notebook, looked at the edge of a sketched map Fatou had helped her draw.

"There's nothing here," she said, flipping to the corner. "Nothing marked."

"Exactly," Jatto said.

They floated in the centre, caught in a current that circled but refused to lead.

Jack looked over the edge of the boat — and frowned.

The water reflected the trees, the boat, and the sky.

But not their faces.

His reflection was missing. Just ripples. As if he were a shadow, the river hadn't decided to remember.

"Pick one," he said quietly.

Jatto didn't move.

Then, after a long moment, he pointed toward the narrowest channel. Almost hidden. It bent hard to the right, overhung with roots that knuckled into the water like broken fingers.

"That one," he said.

Lauren frowned. "Why?"

Jatto pushed the pole down into the muck.

"Because the river wants me to take the easy way. That means it's not the right one."

He shoved off.

The boat turned.

Branches scraped the sides.

And slowly, they disappeared into the channel that wasn't supposed to exist.

The channel narrowed until it could barely be called a river.

The boat drifted between roots and vines so tight they had to duck beneath them. Dragonflies danced above the surface. Mist clung low, a skin of breath above the water.

Lauren sat upright, suddenly still.

Jack noticed it first — the way her body stiffened, her pen held motionless over her notebook.

"What is it?" he asked.

She didn't answer.

Instead, her head tilted slightly, like she was listening to something just behind her ear.

Then, very quietly, she said:

"Do you hear that?"

Jack went still. "Hear what?"

She looked up at him.

"Voices. Speaking. In… I don't know. Not English."

Jatto, at the back of the boat, froze. He didn't ask questions. He just started muttering under his breath — a low chant, rhythmic and constant, not meant for them.

Jack strained his ears.

All he could hear was the water. The creak of wood. The shuffle of birds in the trees above.

Until—

A whisper.

Faint. Curling between branches. "Ko ni ta. Nta fa."

Not loud. Not urgent. Just there.

Jack turned his head sharply — toward the bank.

And then he saw him.

A man, standing just inside the trees. Dark-skinned. Bare-chested. Face obscured by the pattern of light through leaves.

The build — the posture — it was Augustus.

Jack stood.

"Stop the boat."

"Sit down," Jatto snapped.

Jack ignored him. The boat was coasting now, no current to fight. He stepped onto the low side rail, balancing.

Lauren grabbed his arm. "Jack—"

But he was already leaping into the shallow water, boots splashing.

He waded to the bank and scrambled up the muddy rise.

"Augustus?" he called.

Nothing.

Just wind.

The man was gone.

Branches shook, but not from motion. From memory.

Jack reached the spot where he'd stood — saw footprints in the mud. Deep. Real.

He touched them. Still damp.

Then, faint behind him, he heard Lauren calling.

"Jack, come back!"

He looked deeper into the trees.

Nothing.

The footprints led nowhere.

But the river still whispered.

And the air smelled faintly of something he hadn't smelled in a long time.

Augustus's sweat. Sand. Salt. Smoke.

The trees parted like a held breath.

The boat slid out of the narrow clutch of branches into a flooded clearing — wide, quiet, rimmed by towering palms and strangler figs. The light opened above them, pale and diffused like an old photograph.

Jack blinked.

What emerged before them wasn't land. It was a drowned memory.

Old wooden stilts jutted out of the water, some still clinging to the broken bones of huts. Thin slats, black with rot, leaned into the current. Roof frames collapsed inward. Walls were long gone.

Just beneath the surface, Lauren caught the curve of a painted gourd, rocking gently, its ash-grey spirals faint yet visible. Close by, a string of red beads drifted like a water snake, still knotted to the splinters of a fallen post.

"Is this it?" she whispered.

Jatto shook his head.

"No. Not yet. This was before it."

"Before?"

He pointed.

"To reach Ndangan, you pass through its shadow."

The boat coasted slowly through the clearing. Jack stared at the remnants — stilt pylons carved with fading marks, rope charms tangled in branches.

Everywhere, charms.

Hung from posts. Nailed to a floating bark. Made from feathers, fish bones, strips of cloth — small offerings that swayed slightly with the water's breath.

Lauren reached over the edge of the boat and plucked one from the river: a bundle of cloth, wrapped tight, the size of a child's fist. She unrolled it gently.

Inside was a coin. Colonial-era. Rusted almost smooth. The Queen's face eroded to a blank oval.

Jack looked at her. "Someone wanted to be remembered."

Lauren nodded, quietly folding the cloth and letting it back into the water.

The boat passed a tilted shrine — stone and wood, mostly submerged. A carved face stared out from the base, eyes eroded, mouth wide as if caught in an endless chant.

Jack whispered, "This isn't ruin."

Lauren looked at him.

"It's a threshold."

Jatto raised a hand — not to speak, but to stop the boat.

He pointed.

Just beneath the water, through the layer of drifting pollen and rootlight, something angular emerged: a platform, mostly sunken, built of lashed bamboo and palm slats. Collapsed, softened by rot, but still clearly crafted. A place where something sacred had once rested.

Jack leaned over, peering in.

A low wooden structure—too small for a home, too intricate for a raft. It had a carved edge. Symbols along its side. Charred black in places. A funeral platform.

Jatto said nothing.

He simply looked at Jack.

The message was clear.

Jack pulled off his shirt.

Lauren caught his wrist. "What if it's not just a place?"

Jack looked at her. His voice was steady.

"Then I'll know."

He lowered himself over the side. The water was warm and heavy. It pressed in around him like a memory refusing to fade.

He kicked once, then twice, descending.

The light thinned. The colour vanished. The silt rose in clouds as he moved his arms through the murk. Roots trailed like hair around the platform. Algae swirled in ribbons.

Then — beneath a fallen crossbeam — something square. Buried in muck.

Jack reached for it.

Wood. Smooth in the centre, ridged on the sides. He scraped the moss away with his fingernails. Carved letters emerged, burned dark into the wood.

The silt drifted.

And the name appeared:

Augustus Sanyang

Elder. Returned.

Jack stared.

The letters didn't blur. They didn't vanish.

This wasn't imagined.

He clutched the tablet to his chest and kicked for the surface.

Jack burst from the water with a gasp, one hand clutched to his chest.

He pulled himself over the side of the boat, soaked, breathless, eyes wild. Lauren grabbed his arm to steady him, her hands slick against his skin.

He held out the tablet.

The wood glistened. Algae still clung to its corners. The carved name was unmistakable:

Augustus Sanyang

Elder. Returned.

Lauren stared.

Jatto reached for it slowly, as if the object might sting. He ran a finger over the letters without speaking. Then, after a moment, he set it gently at his feet.

He looked out over the water.

"This is the edge," he said. "Of what remains."

Jack wiped his face, heart still thudding. "Then we're close."

Jatto didn't respond.

Neither did Lauren.

The boat drifted slightly — not forward, not backwards — as if the river itself were waiting.

Then came a sound.

A single drumbeat.

Soft, distant.

It rolled through the trees like a low knock on a door no one had built.

Lauren turned sharply.

"Did you hear—?"

Another beat.

Softer.

Then silence.

The kind of silence that follows a name being spoken aloud in a place where names don't belong.

Jack looked at Jatto.

His voice was a whisper now.

"Is that…?"

Jatto said nothing.

He simply picked up the pole.

But he didn't push forward.

Not yet.

Because something was near.

And it was listening.

Chapter 13

The Last Dock

The river widened like it was catching its breath.

After hours of silent current and clinging roots, the trees gave way to a sudden, open pool. Still water. Pale light. The mist hovered close to the surface, rising off the river like a veil not yet lifted.

At the margin, half-veiled by mangrove limbs, a narrow dock jutted out; skeletal planks fixed to rotting supports, scarcely wide enough for a single person. Behind it stood a shrine of stone and bone, rising crookedly, its face smoothed by long years of weather and waiting.

And standing there, barefoot, motionless, was an old man.

He wore a wrap of faded white linen and nothing else. His beard was long, curled into itself. His skin was the shade of river silt. And his eyes — milky, unfocused — stared not at them, but through them.

Still, when the boat drifted close, he raised a hand in greeting.

"You came," he said.

Jatto slowed the boat with a gentle push of the pole.

Jack and Lauren exchanged a look. Neither had spoken. Neither had called out.

The old man tilted his head, listening.

"I heard the fire," he said softly. "I heard it in my bones. That means he came back."

Jack stepped onto the dock, carefully. The wood flexed under him. He kept his eyes on the man's face.

"You're Kemo," Jack said.

The old man smiled.

"And you carry his name."

Jatto stayed in the boat. Lauren climbed out behind Jack, quieter, her eyes never leaving the shrine beyond.

Kemo Ba turned toward the sound of her footsteps. "Three travellers. One ghost. One letter. One name that wouldn't stay buried."

Jack swallowed hard.

Kemo took a step forward, reached blindly, and placed a hand on Jack's shoulder.

"You came through the mouth," he whispered. "Now it's time you learn the story that was swallowed."

Kemo's hut stood just beyond the dock, beneath the twisted arms of a fig tree so ancient it seemed to hold the sky in place.

It was no more than four walls of woven reed and faded tarpaulin, patched in places with plastic sacks. But it was standing. And in the centre of the compound, sunken slightly into the soil, was a shrine — carved of stone and termite-eaten wood, shaped into a river's spiral. Its offerings were long gone. No feathers. No coins. No ash bowls. Just silence and moss.

Inside, the air smelled of clay and old fire.

Jack sat cross-legged near the entrance, the wooden nameplate across his lap.

Kemo lowered himself slowly beside him. His knees cracked like dry branches. Lauren crouched just outside the doorway, notebook forgotten in her lap.

Kemo reached out.

Jack guided his hand gently to the tablet.

As his fingers ran across the wood, they slowed — paused at the carved letters. His lips parted slightly, but he didn't speak. Only his brow furrowed, just once, as if feeling the shape of grief for the first time in decades.

He pressed his palm flat against the name:

Augustus Sanyang

Elder. Returned.

His shoulders shook.

No sound came from him.

Just breath.

Then stillness.

After a long moment, he said, "He was always the one who asked why, even when we were children, why the tide moved in and not out. Why some trees fruit and others flower. Why we buried names."

Jack watched him.

"Why didn't he come back?"

Kemo didn't answer right away.

He reached behind him, to a folded cloth in the corner, and unwrapped a single object:

A fishing hook. Large. Carved from riverbone. The same shape Augustus once wore around his neck.

He held it out.

"I kept this," he said. "So the river wouldn't forget him."

Jack took it carefully, reverently.

"He found me," he said.

Kemo smiled faintly.

"No," he whispered. "He led you."

The fire was shallow, barely more than a whisper of flame under a pot of river water and dried cassava root. It cast flickers of gold on the shrine's hollow face.

Kemo sat next to it, his legs folded like brittle paper. Across from him, Jack and Lauren crouched low. Jatto leaned against the fig tree in silence, his face giving nothing away.

Kemo stirred the pot with a carved wooden stick, the scent of smoke and salt rising around them.

"Ndangan was not always quiet," he began. "It used to sing."

Jack leaned forward. "How many lived here?"

Kemo tilted his head as if listening to ghosts count. "Almost two hundred. Fishers. Weavers. A healer. A firemaker. We had our own water lines, our own school. My father taught us with books the colonials left behind — pages in English, printed in Ghana, meant for someone else."

Lauren asked softly, "Why was it erased?"

Kemo didn't speak for a moment.

Then, calmly: "Because we would not kneel."

Jack frowned.

"The state sent representatives after independence. Promises. Aid. But tied to papers. Registries. Elections we did not vote in. People we did not name. So we said no."

"And they punished you?"

"Not with guns," Kemo said. "With forgetting. They redrew the maps. Shut down the postal boat. Closed our well under 'drought controls.' When the children began coughing from bad water, Augustus said we couldn't stay silent."

Jack felt his hands tighten.

"He left to sell the gemstones," Kemo continued. "He said he'd go to Nouakchott. There was a contact — a broker who promised equipment in exchange for stone. Pipes. Medicine. He carried everything with him."

Lauren glanced at Jack.

"He never came back," Jack said softly.

Kemo stirred the fire once. Twice.

"No," he said. "But I believe he found a way to return."

Jack looked down at the nameplate beside him.

Kemo said, "Names can rot in soil. But they do not die if someone speaks them."

Lauren looked at Jack, then back at Kemo. "Why us?"

Kemo smiled gently, as if it was obvious.

"Because you listened to a man no one else could hear."

Dawn came without colour.

Just a pale thinning of the dark, the sound of frogs retreating, and the soft crunch of Kemo's bare feet on the path.

He walked on ahead, his staff tapping lightly against the mud. Jack kept pace beside Lauren, clutching the cloth-wrapped nameplate tightly to his chest. Behind them, Jatto followed, silent as a shadow, his eyes sweeping the branches above.

They moved through a corridor of mangrove and fig, past carved trees that bore no names, only spirals and fishbones — symbols that meant something once, and still did if you knew how to read them.

Then the trees parted.

A clearing opened before them, not wide, but warm. Sunlight filtered in lazy strips through a canopy of vines. Small reed huts clustered at the edges, some half-collapsed, others still alive with smoke trailing from simple chimneys. Chickens darted across hard-packed earth. Two boys played with sticks beside a half-built canoe.

And at the centre, sitting on a low stone bench, were the elders.

Five of them. Four women. One man. Faces mapped by time, spines curved like bows, hands worn with labour and quiet. Their eyes followed the group but didn't flinch. They had seen strangers before. Long ago.

Kemo raised a hand.

The elders nodded.

Then he turned to Jack and Lauren and said, "Now you'll see what forgetting leaves behind."

They approached.

The oldest woman stood. Her back was bent, but her eyes were sharp. She wore a wrap of dark cloth with silver threads woven through it — faded, but still dignified.

Kemo spoke to her in low Mandinka, a slow river of sound Jack couldn't follow.

She stepped forward.

Her eyes passed over Lauren, paused on Jatto, then landed on Jack.

She studied his face like it was a riddle she'd once solved, long ago, and now only needed to remember.

Then she reached up and touched his cheek.

Her fingers were cold.

She whispered something.

Jack looked to Kemo.

He translated quietly.

"She says: He brought you."

Jack swallowed.

Another elder stood, hands clasped in front of her.

She pointed at the wrapped nameplate in his arms.

Then, in English — cracked but clear — she said:

"Augustus came home."

Night came gently to the grove.

No generators. No electricity. Just the slow bleed of firelight from a central pit, and the quiet rhythm of water against reed walls. The villagers gathered in a semicircle around the flame. Elders. Children. A few others Jack hadn't seen earlier — quiet figures who emerged from the tree line like smoke with faces.

Kemo sat beside the fire, staff across his lap.

The nameplate lay before him, propped against a bowl filled with river ash.

The wrapped gemstones were passed around the circle — each person handling them as if they weighed more than stone. Not one word was spoken until they returned to Kemo.

He looked up.

Then, from somewhere beyond the firelight, a single drumbeat sounded.

Jack flinched.

Another beat followed — low, soft, like a heart starting again.

Then another.

Lauren turned, wide-eyed. "That's the same rhythm we heard before."

Kemo nodded.

"It is the rhythm of remembering."

He looked at Jack.

"You were not meant to keep the stones. You were meant to carry them. Back to here."

The drumbeat continued — now joined by hands striking wood, the gentle shuffle of feet in dust, the rise of an ancient melody hummed beneath the breath. The villagers were singing now. Not words — tones. Shapes of sound older than language itself.

Kemo stood, slowly.

"Now you know his name," he said, voice raised just enough to cut through the chant. "Now the river remembers him."

He tossed a small handful of river ash into the fire. It rose in a silver plume.

Then he stepped back and allowed the song to swell.

Jack looked around — the faces lit by fire, the eyes half-closed in memory, the warmth of something older than mourning. It wasn't a ceremony. It was a reclaiming.

Lauren whispered, "He brought us here."

Jack nodded.

"No," he said. "He brought himself home."

And in that moment, under the trees, under the stars, as the drumbeat echoed across the river, Augustus Sanyang was no longer missing.

He was present.

The path beyond the grove wasn't a path.

It was a memory, softened by time and covered in green.

Kemo walked first, slow but sure, tapping his staff against roots and ridges. Two villagers followed with machetes, not to clear the way, but to whisper through it — slicing just enough to let the others pass. Jack, Lauren, and Jatto moved behind them, single file, ducking beneath vines thick as ropes and fern leaves bigger than their heads.

The air was close. Almost sacred.

Jack's shirt clung to him. Sweat dripped from his chin, but he didn't complain. Neither did Lauren. Every so often, she'd pause to scribble notes, then stop — as if words were suddenly too small for what they were walking into.

They crossed a stream barely wider than a ditch, the water covered in tiny floating leaves and vines that trembled without wind. Jatto murmured something under his breath, the kind of protective phrase he'd stopped saying hours ago but picked up again here.

Then the trees broke.

And the ground dipped.

And they stepped into the buried heart of Ndangan.

Sunken footpaths wove through tall grass and moss-stained stone. The husks of clay ovens sat cracked and half-swallowed by roots. Bamboo fences still leaned between old hut rings, skeletal outlines of homes long reclaimed. Bits of blue fabric clung to a fence post. A cooking pot rusted into the soil.

And there — at the centre — a banyan tree rose out of what once was the council house.

Its trunk had split the stone walls apart over the years, sending roots down like anchors, branches up like questions. One wall still stood — carved with patterns, not writing. Spirals, fish, sunbursts. Silent, deliberate echoes of a language older than paper.

Kemo raised a hand. Everyone stopped.

He turned to Jack.

"Now," he said, "you see what silence cannot take."

Jack took a slow step forward, heart thudding. The village wasn't just abandoned.

It had waited.

It was quiet in the village, but not dead.

Beneath the banyan's shade, the air held a hum — low and warm, like a long-held breath returning to its lungs. Insects whispered under leaves. Distant birds called once, then fell silent.

The villagers moved with purpose. Not hurried. Not reverent. Just deliberate.

One began sweeping the old footpath with a bundle of dried palm fronds.

Another began clearing vines from the edge of a collapsed hut.

Kemo motioned for Jack to follow him.

They stepped carefully through a patch of grass that crunched underfoot, and reached a low stone ring — overgrown, but unmistakable.

In its centre sat the altar stone.

Rectangular. Polished from years of hands resting upon it. Lichen clung to its edges. A few deep grooves were carved along the top — names, in old script, barely visible.

Kemo knelt beside it and ran his fingers along the edges, stopping at each groove like they were braille.

"Each elder leaves a name," he said. "When they return."

Jack stared at the stone.

There was a gap — just before the moss overtook the last few marks. A space large enough for one more name.

"He never came back," Jack said softly.

Kemo nodded. "Not in body. But a name doesn't need a body to return."

Jack pulled the wrapped nameplate from his pack.

He knelt. Unwrapped it slowly.

The wood was still damp from the river. The letters are dark, but unblemished.

AUGUSTUS SANYANG

Elder. Returned.

He looked at Kemo. "Are you sure this is mine to place?"

Kemo tilted his head and smiled faintly.

"No," he said. "It was his. But you carried it farther than we could."

Jack set the nameplate gently across the stone.

It didn't fall. It didn't slide.

It fit.

As if it had always waited for this place.

Lauren stood near the banyan's base, notebook in hand, camera slung from her neck but untouched. She was sketching instead — details of the stone ring, the carved wall, and the play of light filtering through the dense canopy above.

Then she saw him.

A boy — no more than seven — barefoot, with short hair and a small scar on his cheek. He wore a threadbare shirt and no expression at all. He walked up without hesitation and held something out to her.

A folded square of paper.

Worn. Yellowed.

She accepted it gently.

He said nothing. Just turned and walked away.

Lauren opened the paper.

Inside: a photograph.

Faded, wrinkled, edges frayed. A black-and-white image of two boys beside a canoe — one older, lean, upright. The other short, grinning. The older boy wore a thin necklace. Bone hook.

It was Augustus.

Maybe fifteen. Maybe younger.

She felt her breath catch.

Someone had kept this. Hidden it. Protected it. Carried it through the heat and the rot and the rain and silence.

She looked up — but the boy was already gone.

Across the clearing, a small plume of smoke curled upward.

One of the elders was lighting the ancestral fire pit. A circle of stones, some cracked, some marked with tiny spirals and river marks. Ashes from long ago still clung to the cracks in its centre.

A second elder brought dried wood. Another added strips of bark.

Soon, the fire caught.

Smoke rose.

Not fast. Not fierce.

But patient, as if it had never been extinguished — only paused.

Jack stepped beside her.

Lauren handed him the photo.

He stared at it.

Then at the fire.

"It's not a grave," he said quietly. "It's a return."

The fire crackled louder. Somewhere in the trees, the drumbeat began again.

Not urgent.

Just certain.

The village, for the first time in decades, began to breathe.

The fire faded behind him.

Jack wandered through the edges of the old village, alone, following a path that wasn't a path — just the way the grass leaned underfoot, the way the trees opened for someone who listened.

He didn't know what he was looking for.

But the ground seemed to guide him.

He passed the remains of a chicken coop, half-collapsed. A child's stool. A broken water jar with spiral paint still flaking off its curve. Vines draped everything like cautious fingers.

Then came the sound.

A whisper.

At first, he thought it was the wind. Then it formed words.

"I remember now."

A child's voice. Speaking perfect English.

He stopped.

"Who's there?"

Silence.

He stepped forward.

A small hut stood at the edge of the clearing, its roof gone and one wall missing. At its centre was a wide basin — once used for washing, now brimming with leaves and rainwater.

He approached.

Bent.

Looked in.

His own face stared back from the water's surface — dirt-smudged, sunburned, older than he'd ever felt.

But it wasn't just his face.

Behind him — in the reflection — stood Augustus.

Not a ghost.

Not an echo.

Just there.

Still.

Watching.

Jack spun.

No one.

Nothing.

Only the leaves, the empty basin, the stillness.

But the voice came again. Not behind him this time. Inside him.

"You carried me farther than I thought I could go."

Jack's breath caught.

"I thought you weren't real."

A pause.

"I was real enough to be forgotten."

Then silence.

Jack looked back into the basin.

The water had gone still again.

And his face was alone.

Dawn broke grey and gold across the treetops.

The village was quiet now, the fires reduced to ash and breath. Smoke curled lazily above the central pit. The drums had stopped sometime in the night.

Jack sat beneath the banyan, the nameplate resting across his knees again.

Kemo approached slowly, barefoot as always, the carved staff balanced lightly in his hand.

He didn't sit. Just stood in front of Jack, looking with eyes that saw nothing and everything.

"You've seen it now," Kemo said.

Jack nodded.

"You've walked where no one was meant to walk. You've heard the name that was meant to vanish. So tell me—" Kemo leaned slightly closer, "—what will you do?"

Jack didn't answer.

Not at first.

Lauren sat nearby, silent, her camera untouched in her lap. Even she didn't know.

Write the story?

Publish it?

Tell the world about the forgotten village, the ghost of Augustus, the place that resisted being erased?

Or leave it as it was?

Alive.

Unclaimed.

Uncommodified.

Jack reached for the nameplate.

He rose to his feet, crossed the clearing, and placed it gently against the base of the ancestral tree.

It leaned slightly into the roots — as if settling.

Then he stepped back.

Kemo said nothing.

Neither did Jack.

Lauren stood, brushing dust from her hands. She looked at him once — not asking, not needing.

Just understanding.

Jatto stood a few paces away, arms crossed, watching the light shift through the banyan limbs. When Jack looked at him, he didn't move.

He wasn't coming.

Jack understood.

Some stories stay where they began.

Jack and Lauren turned and walked.

No goodbyes.

No final words.

The river met them without a sound, smooth as glass. The boat drifted from shore.

And somewhere behind them, behind the trees and fire and silence, the drums began again.

But softly now.

As if they were being played from inside the river.

Chapter 14

What We Brought Back

England felt colder than he remembered.

Not in temperature — but in sound. No insects humming. No river pushing against the banks. Just the thin rasp of wind across brick and windowpanes, and the occasional cough of traffic seeping through closed blinds.

Jack sat at his desk in the flat, one hand hovering over the keyboard, the cursor blinking in the open document titled simply: Ndangan.

He stared at it for a long time.

Then typed the first line:

There was a village the maps forgot.

Then he stopped.

He reached for the pouch — or tried to. But the desk drawer was empty.

He opened the second drawer.

Nothing.

The gemstones were gone.

He checked his bag, the canvas pocket where he'd last placed them. Still nothing.

They had simply… vanished.

Jack didn't tell Lauren.

She had her own questions.

Across town, she texted him:

Can you look at this?

It was one of her prints from the trip — a frame she was sure she had taken of the banyan tree, with the nameplate resting at its base.

But it was blank.

Just mist. Roots. No nameplate.

She sent another: the council house wall.

Blurred. Almost rubbed out.

A third: the boy with the folded photograph.

Only the trees were visible.

My cards aren't corrupted, she wrote.

They're just... missing pieces like something was erased. But not by me.

Jack stared at the messages, then typed:

Maybe it wanted to stay forgotten.

No reply for a while.

Then:

Or maybe it's safer that way.

He closed the chat window.

Looked at the screen.

The single line blinked up at him.

He highlighted it.

Deleted it.

Closed the document.

Some stories weren't meant to be told in words.

Some were meant to be carried.

The morning was quiet.

Too quiet for London. No sirens. No footsteps on the stairs. No neighbour's radio bleeding through the walls.

Jack rose late.

He padded barefoot across the apartment, still heavy with sleep, and reached for the kettle — when he saw it.

Lying on his writing desk.

Neatly placed.

Still damp, faintly smelling of ash and river mud.

The necklace.

The bone-hook, carved smooth with time, threaded onto the same cracked black cord he'd seen Augustus wear in the desert — and again around Kemo's fingers.

He had left it.

At the base of the banyan.

He was sure.

Absolutely, unquestionably sure.

Yet there it was.

Waiting.

Not hidden. Not tucked away in a coat pocket or forgotten rucksack.

Laid out.

Deliberate.

Jack didn't move at first.

He just stared.

Then, slowly, he reached for it. Touched it.

It was warm.

He didn't tell Lauren.

Didn't take a photo.

Didn't even put it on.

He just held it in his palm, feeling the groove of the carving beneath his thumb.

And that night, when he finally fell asleep—

He heard the river again.

And the boat.

And the hush of trees bending toward water.

The dream came gently, like mist.

Jack stood barefoot on the edge of a riverbank.

Not the Thames. Not the Gambia. Somewhere in between.

The water was glass.

The trees leaned low over the surface, their branches heavy with silence.

He didn't look behind him.

He didn't have to.

"I wondered if you'd come," said the voice.

Augustus.

Jack turned.

He sat cross-legged in the grass, arms resting on his knees, his face untouched by time or hunger. Not the corpse Jack had discovered. Not the hallucination he had chased.

He looked young.

Whole.

Real.

His necklace hung easily across his collarbone.

"I left the necklace," Jack said softly.

Augustus smiled.

"You brought it home."

They sat in silence for a moment, just the two of them and the river that had carried both of them farther than they ever meant to go.

"I keep asking myself if you were ever real," Jack said.

"I was real enough to reach you," Augustus answered.

He plucked a reed from the ground and twisted it between his fingers.

"You brought me farther than death," he said. "Do you know what that means?"

Jack shook his head.

"It means you remembered me into being."

Jack looked down at his hands.

"I don't know what to do with what I saw."

"You already did it."

Jack looked at him. "But no one will know."

Augustus leaned forward.

"You don't have to remember everything," he said. "Just that I was."

The wind stirred the water.

Then Augustus stood, the reed still in his hand, and stepped toward the edge of the bank.

"I'm not waiting anymore," he said.

Jack opened his mouth — to ask something, anything.

But Augustus turned once, smiling, and said:

"Tell the river thank you."

And then he was gone.

No splash.

No sound.

Just gone.

The cursor blinked again.

The screen was empty.

Jack stared at it, then closed the laptop.

He reached instead for his notebook — the old leather-bound one he hadn't touched since the day after the return. It still smelled faintly of fire and mangrove smoke.

He opened to a clean page.

Picked up his pen.

Wrote slowly:

Not a story.

A promise.

Then he closed the cover and didn't open it again.

On the table beside him lay a small cardboard box, taped shut, already addressed.

Inside it: the pouch of gemstones he thought he'd lost. They had reappeared in his coat pocket days after the dream — the same weight, the same red and green glints, the faint smell of river mud still clinging to the cloth.

He hadn't said a word.

He simply wrote an address:

Fatou Bah

Bakau, The Gambia.

No return name.

No return address.

He dropped it at the post office before sunrise and didn't look back.

That night, he opened his desk drawer.

The necklace lay inside — the bone-hook coiled like a question mark.

He didn't wear it.

He didn't need to.

He left it there, resting quietly in the dark, next to the closed notebook and the copy of a map where Ndangan did not appear.

It was a narrow stretch of river near Jack's flat.

Not beautiful. Not wild. Tamed by footpaths and metal railings. Joggers went by. Cyclists. Dog walkers. All moving too quickly to see the stillness in the current.

Jack sat on a bench just off the path, coat zipped to the chin, notebook unopened in his lap.

The water moved slowly today — not sluggish, just intentional. Leaves floated like boats without passengers.

He watched without thinking.

Not remembering.

Not forgetting.

Just being.

A breeze stirred his hair.

He leaned forward, elbows on knees.

Then—

Something shifted across the water.

On the far bank, between two thin birches, a man stood.

Alone.

Still.

Not close enough to see clearly — just tall, dark-skinned, arms crossed, chin tilted slightly like he was reading Jack from a distance.

But Jack knew.

He knew in his bones, the way you know when someone you love enters a room behind you without a sound.

The man didn't wave.

Didn't call out.

Just stood there.

Watching.

Waiting.

Jack didn't smile.

Didn't speak.

He simply nodded.

Once.

And across the river, the man nodded back.

Then he was gone.

Jack leaned back slowly.

The water moved.

Epilogue

Where Names Go

The map on Jack's wall hadn't changed.

It still showed the Gambia River curling inland like a question mark. Still listed the same towns: Basse, Banjul, and Bakau. Still left that long stretch upriver blank.

But now, in the margin—drawn in soft pencil, barely legible unless you stood close—was a single word.

Ndangan.

No lines pointed to it. No coordinates. No border.

Just a name.

On quiet nights, Jack would trace it with his fingertip. Sometimes with the bone-hook in his hand, still never worn, still cold and real.

And in the silence between heartbeats, when the air felt just a little too still—

He'd hear the whisper of water.

Not the Thames.

Not any English river.

But that river.

The one that had carried a ghost across continents, through desert and death and back again—not for salvation, but for remembrance.

Jack never published the story.

But he carried it.

And somewhere, far upriver, deep in the trees, beyond where maps would ever dare to speak—

A fire still burned.

And a name stayed spoken.

Author's Note

Hello,

I am Dan Brown.

I have had the pleasure of going to The Gambia more than once and I have experienced the most wonderfully kind, gentle and beautiful people that live there.

Ndangan is a real place. It means 'fishing-place' in the language of the native Serer tribe.

It is a small remote settlement in The Gambia, originally established by Senegalese refugees in 1967. It's located near the River Gambia and is known for its proximity to a large dumpsite. It is home to primarily Gambians with school-aged children.

Over time, Ndangan's area has been reduced due to encroachment by commercial developers who have been allocated land in the area.

The residents' only access to clean drinking water has been the result of the efforts of a charity project, namely Child Aid Gambia.

The settlement is accessed by a small road squeezed between commercial buildings, further limiting access to the community.

The residents face seasonal challenges such as flooding during the wet season and abject poverty, forcing even the youngest children to scour over the nearby dumpsite for plastic bottles, etc., to exchange for very small sums of money.

Despite all their life challenges, visiting this small settlement immerses you in the most gentle, happy people.

It seems that having nothing doesn't diminish the human spirit. If anything, lessons can be learned from those less fortunate.

Ndangan, 'The Forgotten Village', is managed by their youngest village elder. His name is Augustus Sanyang. He is the 'Youngest Alkalo'. A young man focused on the welfare of all the villagers' well-being. He puts their needs before his own every day. He is slowly going blind due to Glaucoma, yet he doesn't let that sway him in his elected role for the village.

He is a man of great principle and moral fibre. To this day, he continues to serve the people of Ndangan the best he can.

On our next visit, we will be taking basic supplies to assist with their small school, like solar-powered calculators, books, pens, etc. Also, anything solar related to help provide free energy and lighting.

Should you, or anyone you know, feel the desire to visit and/or help this wonderful community, your help would always be greeted with thanks and love.